WESTERN

SLATTERY STANDS ALONE

SLATTERY STANDS ALONE

Steven C. Lawrence

Chivers Press • G.K. Hall & Co.
Bath, Avon, England • Thorndike, Maine USA

This Large Print edition is published by Chivers Press, England, and by G.K. Hall & Co., USA.

Published in 1997 in the U.K. by arrangement with the author's estate

Published in 1996 in the U.S. by arrangement with Lawrence A. Murphy.

U.K. Hardcover ISBN 0–7451–4937–5 (Chivers Large Print)
U.K. Softcover ISBN 0–7451–4948–0 (Camden Large Print)
U.S. Softcover ISBN 0–7838–1848–3 (Nightingale Collection Edition)

The text of this Large Print edition is unabridged.
Other aspects of the book may vary from the original edition.

Set in 16 pt. New Times Roman.

Printed in Great Britain on acid-free paper.

British Library Cataloguing in Publication Data available

Library of Congress Cataloging-in-Publication Data

Lawrence, Steven C.
  Slattery stands alone / Steven C. Lawrence.
  p. cm.
  ISBN 0–7838–1848–3 (lg. print : sc)
  1. Large type books. I. Title.
[PS3562.A916S56 1996]
813'.54—dc20   96–20885

CHAPTER ONE

'There they come,' Robby Malmgren said. He stood from the cane-bottom chair he had tilted back against the rough boarding of the Rapahoe Saloon porch wall. Robby was tall for twenty, long and thin, yet he was still two inches under his brother Jake's six-four. Jake, standing just outside the green-painted batwings, spoke softly. 'Hold it down, kid. O'Hearn'll see them. He'll be across.'

Robby said, 'Ain't nothin' wrong with you tellin' Shields they're comin'.'

Jake Malmgren pushed the left half of the slatted swinging doors out and stepped down alongside his brother. 'You hold it. There'll be talk once we pull it. I don't want Shields tyin' any of us in when he thinks back to the stage comin'.'

He pushed his sombrero high on his black curly hair and wiped the sleeve of his faded gray shirt across his sweaty forehead. Directly opposite them the jail door was wide open. Hager had been looking out most of the morning, and the damn fool would pick right now to clean the bed pots or spittoons or do some other useless grubby job for the sheriff. The big Concord stage was already a quarter down the switchback road that wound like a snake from the southeast pass. The only other

1

wagon in sight was LeDuc's old buckboard. The Frenchman had come in before eight to do his buying early. That way he got himself and his half-Indian daughter out of town ahead of the time when the saloon and Whitey's store got into full swing. Jake watched the stubby, bearded squawman and the black-haired girl beside him. So damned hot for May, and the Frenchie still wore that checkered red and black lumberjack shirt.

'Hager's lookin' out,' Robby remarked quietly. His careful blue eyes flicked from the jail doorway to the switchback road. LeDuc's wagon was still a half mile below the Concord. The sun, two hours above the eastern rim, shined like white silver off the snow patches left along Mount Washburn's peak. The crest of the Tetons far to the southwest was as clear as he'd ever seen. The air was full of a warm, melting pine smell. 'We couldn't get a better day for it.'

'Day's just as good for Shields,' Jake said. He touched his brother's shoulder, warning him to be quiet. O'Hearn had appeared from the jail. The lawman wore only his sixgun and for a brief instant Jake Malmgren wished he'd decided to hit the stage right there in Beaver Hole. The thought vanished when he followed O'Hearn's stare.

'Six of them,' he said to Robby. 'There's one inside the stage.' He nodded at the Concord. Sunlight glinted off the sight of a rifle barrel

2

that jutted out the left window. 'That Slattery's what Quinn says he is. Damn careful man.'

'He's on the black in front,' said Robby. 'Quinn knew—' He quieted as the sheriff reached the bottom step and Jake asked, 'You're goin' to meet the shipment, Dan? You want Robby to go with you?'

Dan O'Hearn took two long-legged strides onto the porch and halted beside the brothers. He was as big and heavy-set as Jake. The tied-down .44 Colt was as much a part of the lawman as his right hand which swung freely close to the weapon's bone handle. 'No,' he told them. 'Slattery'll keep it till Charlie takes over.' He moved to push past the batwings.

Jake Malmgren followed the lawman. 'Robby's goin' to be one of the guards, Dan. He could beat Charlie's wagon.'

O'Hearn paused with his hand against the slats and spoke across his shoulder. 'Okay, go ahead, Robby,' he said. 'Have Meric swing into the road.'

'Sure. I'll tell him.' Robby hesitated long enough to see his brother's nod before Jake followed the sheriff inside. The first part was almost over and everything had gone without a hitch. Jake had gotten Robby the job of riding shotgun for Shields' money. He'd be right with the shipment at Charlie Shields' back if anything went wrong. But nothing could go wrong, not after Jake had set up the plan with Quinn. Quinn had known right from the day

3

Shields agreed to sell the eight-hundred head of cattle to Slattery. Quinn had mailed Shields' letter in Cody last month and he'd read about the shift of the twelve-thousand cash from the Concord to the Shields' buggy. It was Jake who'd made Quinn find out what he could about Slattery. Jake had heard the name down on the Rio Bravo the year before. There had been a shootout with a gang of gunrunners and a near lynching, and a fast gun called Slattery had been connected to both. If Jake hadn't made Quinn check, they'd have tried hitting the stage the other side of Mile High Pass. With two guns on the stage seat and three riders it was enough, but Slattery had at least one gun inside. Maybe more...

'What in hell?' Robby Malmgren muttered to himself. He halted in the middle of the roadway. He felt the breeze, cool against his beardless face now that he was clear of the buildings. LeDuc's buckboard had stopped up there beyond the marshy green stretch of meadow. The Concord had almost reached the Frenchie, and the riders were pulling in close to the wagon. Robby Malmgren turned, realizing the stupid squawman had gotten stuck where the switch-back had been gutted by the run-off from the winter storm. Robby could see the dark shine of little rivulets of water trickling down from the spot. He could see the meadowlarks and jays swooping up and flashing through the sunlight in long, graceful dives. He could see as clearly the stage wouldn't get to town until the buckboard was freed. That could throw the whole holdup plan off since Rachins and Keelin were waiting. Robby hurriedly retraced his steps toward the porch of the saloon so he could get inside and tell Charlie Shields and let his brother know.

* * *

Tom Slattery glanced back at the huge Concord stage. The driver had turned the reins around the brake handle and was getting ready to climb off. Beside him the shotgun guard laid his double-barreled Greener flat on the board seat.

'No, stay up there,' Slattery told them. 'Lute, Dave, don't show yourselves.' He watched the two rifles pull into the stage windows, then returned his eyes to the mired-down wagon. He'd already seen that the rear left axle had cracked from the vehicle's entire weight being thrown onto it when the rim had struck the rut. The driver, wearing a checkered shirt, was a stubby, heavy-set man with a thick black beard and a complexion as dark as Augustin Vierra's. The girl beside him was no more than eighteen. Her hair was as black. She had on a dark blue dress. Her face was small and round. Long fine lashes ringed her deep-set black eyes. The driver spoke quickly to her. She'd been watching Slattery and Augustin

5

pull in alongside their wagon horse. She looked away while she stood to get off the seat.

The driver snapped his whip across his gray's flank. The horse snorted and strained in the harness, but the buckboard didn't budge.

'You'll need a pull,' Slattery told him. He eased forward in the saddle while he took his lariat from the horn. He was a big man, thick through the chest and shoulders. His flat-crowned gray hat was tugged down low over his forehead, partially hiding his long stubbled jawline. He and Vierra and the two riders who'd stayed alongside the Concord had guarded the twelve-thousand dollars the entire distance from Montana to Wyoming Territory, and he didn't completely trust this breakdown. The girl was too guarded in her glances, the driver too openly showing them he wanted no help.

Slattery's gaze flicked around the Concord, then up into the pass. Mal Weaver, leading Lute Canby's and Dave McPeck's mounts, was in sight at the foot of the slot. Nothing else moved close by. Below, in the small town, men had poured out of the saloon. Most were climbing onto horses. The growth of timber alongside the creek that cut the Hole from the western pass blocked a full view of the lower end of the valley. A small pressure of one knee made Slattery's black gelding swing its rump to the left onto solid ground to give its hoofs firm footing.

'Catch,' Slattery told the driver. 'Hook on and I'll take the strain.'

The driver shook his head. He whipped the horse again, but the animal's pulling did no good.

Augustin Vierra moved his bay stallion in next to the seat. He looked from the driver to the girl. 'Get down with her, senor. Without your weight—'

'I can do this myself,' the black bearded man snapped.

'No, you cannot, senor,' Augustin answered. Slattery held the coil above his head. 'Catch it, mister,' he ordered. 'I don't want to be stopped in the open like this.' He swung the lariat and let the noose go toward the driver.

The driver caught the hemp rope. Reluctantly he turned it about the iron supports of the seat. Augustin had his coil ready. He rode past the girl, who watched calmly. Her face showed nothing, was neither friendly nor unfriendly. The dark-skinned Mexican hooked his noose around the wagon's rear, backed his mount, and took the strain with Slattery.

Easily, slowly, the iron wheel rim came up from the mud, one inch, another, then suddenly broke loose with a loud sucking noise. The wagon rolled ahead and stopped, tilted a bit to the left on the weakened hub.

Slattery slackened up on the line. He began to coil it as he rode to the door. 'You won't get

7

far on that,' he said. 'Not till it's fixed.'

The bearded man gave no answer. He stepped to the ground and walked back to look at the damaged wheel. Hoofbeats drummed on the roadway below them. The six riders who approached were led by a man of about fifty who sat squat in the saddle, his jowly face burned brick-red from a lifetime of working cattle. He wore a wide Spanish sombrero and a long black frock coat. His pale, hostile eyes watched the bearded driver long before he reined in.

'What in hell you pullin', LeDuc?' he called. 'Blockin' the road like that?'

'My wheel got caught, Mr Shields,' Eduard LeDuc said. He motioned for the girl to climb aboard. 'I was taking my daughter to Cody.'

'You picked a right good time for it.' Charles Shields walked his roan mare past the wheel, seeing that it was ready to buckle at any moment. 'Pull over so's the stage can pass. Come on, get over.'

'I am, Mr Shields.' The girl was in the seat. Her father took hold of the side of the snaffle bit and began to turn his horse to go down the switchback.

Shields edged his mount ahead, toward Slattery. The rancher offered his right hand. 'Sorry this had to happen,' he said loud enough for LeDuc to hear. 'You should have ridden right over that fool squawman.' He studied the Concord while he gripped Slattery's fingers.

8

'You had this money covered all right.' He grinned at the two men hidden inside the box.

Slattery said, 'My neighbors mortgaged every foot of land to borrow enough for your cows. There's more than money with us.'

Shield's grin held. He motioned around at the riders with him. 'I told Jake Malmgren about you losin' all that beef in the freeze. He's got a deal for you.'

The rider directly behind him, a tall and strong-faced man, took his eyes off the wagon LeDuc had stopped on a wide section of road. His leather skin wrinkled when he gave a quick grin. 'You want more cattle, Slattery,' he said, 'I'll get it for you.'

'Oh, no you don't,' Shields cut in. 'Not till I sign my beeves over to him at the buggy.' He nodded to the town and the covered surrey that had been driven out from behind the buildings and waited in the shadows at the west end. 'You can talk business after that.'

Malmgren laughed good-naturedly and swung his long-legged gray gelding with Shield's roan. The grin was still there as he glanced back at Slattery. 'You give Charlie his money,' he said. 'I got a kid brother who's drawin' wages guardin' it. You see to Charlie and we'll go over the Rapahoe and have some grub.'

Without waiting for an answer, Malmgren spurred his horse out ahead of Shields. Slattery waved the stage driver on, then fell in with

9

Augustin Vierra. The word of the deep freeze which had killed most of the cattle in Montana the last winter had spread fast. It was known that he and the other ranchers from Calligan Valley were in the market for all the restocking cattle they could afford. Slattery thought fleetingly of the three-thousand head they'd lost, the day-after-day job they'd had getting rid of the carcasses they'd found under the twenty foot drifts of snow once the Chinook thaw set in. If Malmgren or anyone else would sell more stock at fifteen dollars a head, he'd come back during the summer.

They reached the LeDuc wagon. Slattery slowed King to allow the Concord to squeeze past. The bearded driver and his daughter sat motionless on the seat. Both watched Shields and the men with him. Fear was in their postures. It had been in LeDuc's voice when he'd spoken to the rancher. Augustin Vierra stopped near Slattery, his attention on the girl. Her dark hair fell about her shoulders and hid her eyes. There was no perceptible rise and fall of her firm round bosom under her thin blouse. She gave no indication she was aware of being watched, but she knew.

Slattery and Augustin followed behind the stage-coach, riding slowly in its dusty wake. For the first time since they'd stopped, Slattery felt the cool breeze that blew across the western peaks. He took off his flat-crowned hat and brushed a hand through his black hair. The heads of a few clouds showed beyond the far pass, the hazy grayish clouds that came with springtime heat. They could pile up over Washburn Peak and a storm would give them trouble moving the herd out of the Hole. But there was little chance. They lay so still, and the sky was so clear and blue directly overhead.

'Thank you,' LeDuc said from the wagon as they passed, 'for helping us pull out.'

Both Slattery and Augustin looked around. The bearded Frenchman was swinging his horse in behind them. He nodded. His daughter still gave them no attention. She stared up at the pass, her pretty features sullen and without warmth.

'That is all right, senor,' Augustin Vierra answered while Slattery nodded. They followed the Concord into the valley, hearing the broken wagon wheel creek, rumble and squeak behind them until they moved beyond earshot to the level, smoother roadway which had been cut through the lush green of the meadows.

* * *

Charles Shields had his surrey waiting in the middle of the wide roadway. Beaver Hole was much larger than the small town Slattery had left five days earlier. Where Yellowstone City was a group of wooden buildings clustered around a single four corners, here Center

11

Street stretched longer than a hundred yards, with three side streets leading to the residential sections behind the false-fronted business district. Slattery kneed King ahead of the Concord once they reached the land and mining claims office and livery barn at the eastern limits. Three women and a white-haired old man came out of the general store to watch. Some boys who played kick-the-can paused at the mouth of the middle cross street. A small, skinny deputy with a star on his white shirt stepped through the jail doorway and stood on the walk. The deputy did not carry a rifle, nor did he wear a holstered sixgun. The only other lawman in view was big and heavy-set. He held a long-barreled Winchester. His sheriff's badge glinted in the sunlight while he waited with Shields and the four armed riders who guarded the surrey.

Shields waved to the youngest of the guards as the stage slowed to a stop. 'Robby, you and Quinn give a hand puttin' the money into the buggy.' He stood aside while the driver and shotgun rider strained to lift the square iron box with a large iron lock on it from beneath the seat. Lute Canby, his round bald head shiny in the sunlight, pushed open the stage door. He stepped out, followed by the thinner, taller Dave McPeck. Mal Weaver, leading both Canby's and McPeck's horses, was approaching the men and motionless vehicles. He rode easily in the saddle, glancing carefully from side to side at those who'd come out to watch.

Shields laughed. 'Your man doesn't trust this,' he said to Slattery. His gaze flicked from the rifles Canby and McPeck carried to his own guards. 'Wasn't one chance anyone could hit you people. Won't be any danger now that we've got it.'

Slattery nodded to Sheriff O'Hearn. 'You're going along?'

The lawman shook his head. Shields answered for him. 'No need for Dan to come any further than the town limits. I'll have four men with me. Six, once Lewis and Patton get back from the herd.'

'Then the money's yours.' Slattery had watched the pair Shields had called Robby and Quinn, both straining while they set the strongbox on the surrey's front seat. 'You going to count it?'

Still smiling, Shields answered, 'Don't have to. Your word's good enough for me. Now, you want to sign the bill of sale, I'll have Quinn take you out to the herd.'

Jake Malmgren, standing directly behind Shields, said, 'How about the offer I made, Slattery? I'd like to talk it over with you before you go out.' When Slattery looked at Augustin Vierra, Malmgren added, 'It won't take long. If you need more cattle, I can get them for you.'

One of Shield's cattlehands had led the rancher's roan in close to the surrey. The

13

rancher put his boot into the stirrup and swung up into the saddle. 'It'll take a half, three-quarters of an hour for me to get out to the herd,' he told Slattery. 'Your crew could be cuttin' the steers you want. I'll bring the papers out there.'

Slattery nodded. The eight hundred he'd get from Shields would barely begin to replace the three thousand he and his neighbors in Montana needed. He would either have to go back to Texas and spend time on a gather and drive or build up a steady supply of steers from this territory. He said to Vierra, 'The four of you start moving the herd. I'll be out before you trail them.'

'We will, Tomas,' said the Mexican.

Shields spoke to the cowhand who'd helped with the strongbox. 'You go with them, Quinn. Remember, they cut every head they want.'

'Yes sir, Mr Shields.' He was strongly built, wide in the shoulders and across the back. His darkly tanned face turned to Vierra. 'Just follow me. The herd's due north.'

Canby and McPeck had mounted beside Weaver. They walked their horses behind Augustin Vierra toward where Quinn's stallion was tied at the gun shop hitchrail. Shields pulled ahead of the surrey and said to the driver and four guards, 'All right. Keep your eyes open. We go straight to the house.'

Dan O'Hearn took a few steps alongside the rancher's roan. 'You sure you don't want me to

14

go along, Charlie?'

'No. We don't need you.' He stared around at the deputy. 'You don't want to leave Alfie alone, Dan.'

Jake Malmgren laughed along with the others within hearing. Only O'Hearn didn't laugh. The lawman stood in the street watching the surrey and horsemen head westward. Malmgren, drawing his horse on its bridle like Slattery, took a stride in the direction of the Rapahoe Saloon.

'How many more head you figure you can take?' he asked Slattery.

'Maybe five hundred by fall. I'll know better after next winter.'

Jake Malmgren nodded and said, 'If I have them driven to your valley, price'll be higher than the fifteen you paid Shields.'

They had reached the steps of the saloon. Slattery paused to turn a halter knot around the worn pine post. He gazed toward the north. His riders who'd gone with Quinn were moving at a lope and were already out of sight. The grass of the broad stretch of meadow was bending in wide open spots under the wind, the low areas dark like waves, the rest shining under the sun when the strong gusts eased up. The clouds which had piled up over Mount Washburn had blown out toward the Hole, shading the timberline that traced the long sweep of the river. Shields' surrey had crossed to the opposite bank, only its black top was

15

visible. Sheriff O'Hearn was walking toward the deputy.

Slattery asked, 'How much more?'

'Wal—' Malmgren was thoughtful while he stepped up onto the porch. 'I'd say seventeen, eighteen dollars a head.' He moved to the double doors, hesitating until Slattery reached him. 'I'll tell you what, you deliver the money like today, my price'll be fifteen, same as Charlie's.'

'Fair enough,' Slattery said. Malmgren pulled the left door out to let Slattery enter the barroom first.

The gunfire broke out at that instant. A confused, loud, quick banging of many weapons. The staccato cracks echoed along the meadows into the town and off the line of buildings. Malmgren ran across the porch and down the steps. Slattery, a stride behind him, had his .44 Colt drawn from beneath his waistband. O'Hearn, his sixgun also in hand, was in the middle of the roadway fifty yards ahead of them.

Echoing gunblasts died under the shouts and calls of the men, women and children who poured from the doorways. The quick eruption of shots fell off to a single bang, then silence from the line of trees that blocked the surrey from view.

Malmgren ran fast, completely shocked at what had happened. The men he had waiting were three miles out, well clear of town and any

16

chance of Dan O'Hearn going after them. He called loudly to the lawman. 'Dan! Go in straight, Dan! We'll head for the bend!'

O'Hearn didn't turn or answer. A hundred feet from the screening timber, he kept running straight and tall, his sixgun out in front of him.

'Cut left, Slattery!' yelled Malmgren. 'Left! I'll cover you!'

The single shot that exploded from the thick growth of brush and trees at the river bend below them drove both men into a crouch. O'Hearn fell forward as though he'd tripped. He rolled over, shouted back to Slattery and Malmgren. 'I'm hit! Watch it! He'll get you! Watch the bend!'

The hidden rifle slammed again. Slattery heard the bee-buzz of the slug burn between Malmgren and himself. He couldn't see the bushwhacker, caught only a flash of red color low in the trees. He aimed and fired once, zig-zagging to make a poorer target.

Horses hoofs clomped beyond the river ford, the noise as loud and confused as the outbreak of gunfire had been. Slattery and Malmgren moved past O'Hearn. The lawman, still sprawled flat, his left hand gripping his torn, bloody pantsleg, waved them on. 'Watch it! Watch the trees!'

The drumming of hoofs moved away while Slattery and Malmgren ran ahead. Yells came from the town. Quick, loud shouts rose from the trees in front of them.

17

They saw the surrey before they'd splashed across the shallow ford, their boots kicking up water onto their trousers. The only horse in sight was the one harnessed to the surrey. Four men stood looking down at a fifth. Charles Shields straightened when he heard the steps. The fingers of his right hand were red with blood where he tried to stop the flow that oozed from a wound in his left shoulder.

'They got the money!' he called. 'Five, six of them!' He took a single step toward Malmgren, then halted. 'Jake, they shot Robby.'

Malmgren's shocked 'No!' silenced the group. He moved ahead of Slattery, past the surrey to where his brother lay. 'Charlie? How?'

'Five of them were waitin' in the trees!' the rancher told him. 'They rode out with their guns on us! We didn't have a chance!'

'They made us get off our horses and throw our guns in the crick,' a lean, rawboned cowhand named Lew Gassen added. 'They knocked off the lock and stuffed the money into saddlebags. They took our horses with them.'

'The kid.' Malmgren edged past the men and stared down at his brother. Robby Malmgren lay flat on his back, a small bullet hole that hardly showed blood in the middle of his chest. A second slug had struck his left hand, a third his right leg. 'How come only him?'

Charlie Shields said, 'He tried to grab one of

18

their guns when they started to ride. I couldn't stop him, Jake. I tried, but he got the gun and fired. I was so close to him, they hit me too.'

'The one at the bend hit him first,' Gassen said angrily. 'He was hid there and he hit Robby 'fore he had a chance to shoot more 'n once.'

'I saw him,' one of the others said. 'He wore a red and black shirt. You remember LeDuc? He drove that damned wagon of his 'round back of town.'

Slattery asked, 'You saw him? You could identify them?'

'Only that damned Frenchman,' Gassen snapped. 'They all had bandannas tied up over their faces.'

'But you saw this LeDuc?'

'We saw him all right,' Shields said. 'He had on that red shirt. We saw that.'

'Damned right,' Gassen added. 'We'll get a posse. String that one up!'

Slattery looked at the willows and alders and cottonwoods along the river bend, the thick growth deeply shadowed about a hundred yards from where the surrey had stopped. 'Look, you better be sure—'

'Sure! What do you mean "sure"!' Jake Malmgren bent over his brother and snarled, 'He killed the kid! They seen him! He was the one who hit O'Hearn. You saw where he was!'

Slattery shook his head. 'He was too far away. I couldn't say for certain.'

'Charlie's certain!' Malmgren snapped. 'So's Lew and Meric and Yeager.' He straightened slowly, his expression suddenly changed. He spoke quietly, but his voice was just as biting and deadly. 'You stopped for his wagon, Slattery. He got a look at the strongbox.'

'His wheel was broken.'

'Just at the right spot,' Malmgren said. 'He had time to talk to you. He had time, Slattery.' His eyes flashed to his dead brother, then returned to Slattery. 'We're goin' after that squawman, mister, and you're comin' with us. He was the one who killed that poor kid! He's damned well gonna swing for it!'

CHAPTER TWO

'Hold on, Alf,' Dan O'Hearn said angrily. The small, skinny deputy had run out after the shooting and had been the first to reach the sheriff. Alf had supported O'Hearn's elbows while the bigger, heavier man had pushed himself up from the ground. Behind them the whole town had poured out. Men ran toward them to help, while the women hung back holding their excited sons and daughters close to them. Slattery and Charlie Shields had appeared across the shallow river ford. The cattlehands who'd guarded the strongbox walked a few feet behind them, talking to Jake

20

Malmgren. Last came the surrey, moving slowly. The man slumped over beside the driver was Robby Malmgren. The sheriff knew Robby was dead. Even at this distance he could tell that. Once more he tried to set his weight carefully on the wounded leg, but, as it had the first time he'd tried, the leg buckled and he grabbed for Alf's arm. 'Hold me! Dang it, Alf! Straighten up!'

'You're so heavy, Mr O'Hearn.'

'Keep me straight! Don't let me fall!' O'Hearn wondered now why in the world he'd ever taken this skin-and-bones on as deputy in the first place. Because he'd married Alf's cousin, and no one else in the Hole would hire him ... because there'd never been a shootout or holdup in the town before.

Fred Johnson, the fat gunsmith, and two other men approached the sheriff. 'Fred!' O'Hearn called. 'Get on my left side! Keep me up! Come on, Fred!'

Slattery was halfway across the ford. Shields talked in a streak to the tall cattleman and held his left shoulder. Only two of them had been hit. That's all, O'Hearn thought. With Alf and Johnson supporting him, he hopped forward to meet Slattery and Shields. Here he was— sheriff—the one in charge of keeping the law, and he hadn't even gotten to the crick once the shooting broke out—

'Dan! They got my money!' Charlie Shields called before he reached the lawman. 'They

21

killed Robby!'

'There were five of them!' Jake Malmgren shouted so the men who crowded in from the walks could hear. 'We seen one, that squaw-lovin' Frenchie, LeDuc! He killed my brother! He was the one who hit Dan, too!'

'That's right,' Lew Cassen yelled. 'We saw him! Get your horses! We'll get them! Every one of them killers!'

The talk that erupted calmed when Dan O'Hearn spoke. He had been looking beyond the mountains at the dark clouds. 'Bring warm clothes,' he told the men. 'We'll be out a longtime in that weather.'

'We will, Dan,' a man said.

'Don't worry, Sheriff! We know what to do!' another put in. 'When we get that Frenchie, we'll know what to do!'

Slattery wanted to speak to the lawman, but the crowd closed in around O'Hearn and the two who helped support him. It would do no good to try calling to the men who ran toward their homes for weapons and warm clothing. He'd seen their faces, every one of them set and angry. The remarks they shouted to each other were furious and hate-filled. Slattery moved into the center of the town, swept along with the excitement which had gone through the whole village. Women and children waited on every porch and in the doorways of houses. Small boys who'd broken away from their mothers scurried alongside the men, calling

22

questions. A few followed the surrey, looking up at the dead man on the seat while they asked the driver about the shooting.

Slattery's gelding waited at the saloon hitchrail. Jake Malmgren stepped beside the black to untie his horse. 'I'm gonna help get the rest of the mounts from the livery,' he told Slattery. 'You'll be waitin' at the jail?'

Slattery nodded. 'I want Gus Vierra and the others to know about this. You want the sheriff to have Shields' men brought in too?'

'Don't worry 'bout that. I've already sent word out. I just want to be sure you're comin'.' Malmgren had his gray clear of the hitchrail. He climbed into the saddle and headed for the livery.

Slattery walked King diagonally across to the jail. Two mounted men, both holding carbines, rode in from the first cross street. Others were visible in front of their homes, the women of the town staying with their men, and all as stirred up as the husbands and fathers of Beaver Hole. Slattery didn't miss the shouting which went on, someone telling a neighbor the livery was letting horses free to anyone that joined the posse, or where an extra gun or heavy coat could be secured. Slattery knew each man who came along would stick to the end. Robbery and killing in such a quiet town, so viciously done, was an outrage. Men that hadn't used a gun except to hunt jack rabbits or deer didn't back out of something like this once they got started.

The sheriff's office was a large room with whitewashed stone walls and spotless pine floorboards. Alf Hager kept everything as neat and clean as would a tidy housewife. Papers on the rolltop desk were arranged in a neat pile beneath a bone ashtray. The gunrack, next to a bulging bookshelf, was well dusted, the line of rifles and shotguns oiled and polished until they shone with a dull bluish sheen. O'Hearn sat on a cane-bottom chair just inside the cellblock corridor. His wound was worse than Slattery had thought. Where Hager had cut away the bloody pantsleg, the entire top and inner round of the thigh was swollen and still oozing blood. Alf had taken the sheet from the first cell and was tearing it into long strips of bandage.

'It'll stop,' the sheriff was saying. 'Wrap it up and it'll stop.'

'I don't think it will,' Alf Hager answered. 'It'll open up if you try ridin'.' His long, thin face turned toward the sound of Slattery's footsteps. 'He can't ride with that leg. He can't even stand on it.'

O'Hearn said angrily, 'What do we do then, Alfred? Let you lead the posse?' He stared down at the wound as Hager silently dropped to his knees and tied the bandage on the leg.

Slattery said, 'Sheriff, I'm not sure LeDuc was the one who shot you. I couldn't see that good.'

24

'Well, I could,' the lawman said testily. 'Tighter, Alf.' He grimaced at the pain. 'I saw his shirt. That's good enough for me.'

'Sheriff, you went down before you could see him. I couldn't see him.'

'Listen, Slattery. Robby Malmgren was born and raised in this town. He was a good kid. He and Jake have had it bad the last few years and they've practically lost everythin' their Paw left them. I'm not standin' for anyone comin' into this valley and tellin' me how to handle our troubles.'

'I'm not telling you how to run things. I don't want to see a man lynched—'

'Nobody's gonna get lynched. Not by my posse.' O'Hearn's jaw suddenly stiffened and he grabbed at his leg. 'Easy! Easy, Alf! There's a bone in there that got hit!' Pain cut deep lines into the edges of his mouth, tightening his jowls. 'Charlie and the rest of them saw LeDuc. He'll swing with the rest of that gang. I want every one of them that killed that boy out there.'

'For trial, Sheriff?'

'Yes, dammit, for trial.' He raised his eyes and stared through the open doorway. Eight riders were out there and another joined while he looked. The mutter and movement which went on was loud but controlled. The serious, tight faces watched the office, waiting. O'Hearn shook his head as though he fought to keep his strength. But his voice seemed weak and tired. 'Get out and tell them to line up for the oath, Slattery. I'll be right out and we'll get started.'

* * *

From the livery barn work area Jake Malmgren saw Gil Rachins ride into town. Jake had spent the past three minutes helping Dunbar, the hostler, saddle fresh horses for the posse. Jake wasn't chancing one thing. He'd planned the holdup that had never come off because another bunch had hit the surrey first. He'd lost his brother in a useless, senseless killing. But he had a line on the gang that did it. The more he thought of it, the more he was certain LeDuc had faked that breakdown up on the switch-back so he could check on the strongbox. Slattery had gone along with the Frenchie's trick so openly, Jake wondered now if Slattery had been a part of the plan. He could've been, which was exactly why Jake hadn't sent anyone after Slattery's Mex friend and his other riders. He'd have someone do that later, after the posse was far enough ahead. They'd have Slattery with them in the posse, and if he was in it with LeDuc, they'd swing together. Jake was thinking of this when he spotted Rachins break through the river brush and lope across the shallows.

'Get over to the jail,' Malmgren called to the men who were still inside the barn tightening their cinches. 'I'll meet you down there. Hurry up!'

He heard 'We're comin', Jake,' and 'Be right with you,' while he spurred his gray gelding ahead. Rachins was moving past the line of storage sheds at the western limits. He wanted to meet his man before anyone else had a chance to answer any questions.

Jake rose up in the stirrups, waving his arm in the air. 'Gil.'

Rachins rode directly to him and asked, 'What happened, Jake? We saw six riders hightailin' it away from here.'

Malmgren moved to draw the rider over to the far side of the roadway, but old Calvin Hall, passing on his horse, caught what had been said. Hall was past seventy-five, his short and narrow body so round-shouldered and bent he was nearly hunchback. He waved his ancient Springfield toward the jail. 'Hey! Gil saw that gang that killed Robby! They passed him and he saw them!'

Men who heard Hall crowded in around the three horses. Rachins eyed them, his square-jawed, stubbled face careful. 'They were too far off to make out. But there were six of them.'

'Did one of them have a red shirt on?' Malmgren asked.

Rachins nodded and Malmgren said, 'That was LeDuc. He was the one who shot Robby. You see which way he went?'

'They were all stayin' in close to the river.'

27

He meant to say more, but the talk that started grew louder. Jake Malmgren shouted, 'They were headin' for LeDuc's! They'll be held up tryin' to take the girl with them! Get over and get sworn in! We'll stop them!'

Horses and riders and the men who'd stopped to listen on the boardwalk swung in one large group across toward the jail. Rachins edged his horse in closer to Malmgren. 'Everythin's off then, Jake. I'll have to tell Reno and Keelin.'

'Get them. Bring them in so they can join the posse.'

Malmgren glanced at the jail doorway. Slattery had appeared. Directly behind him Dan O'Hearn, with Alf Hager and Fred Johnson holding him up, was coming through the doorway. 'I'm sorry 'bout the kid, Jake,' Rachins said. 'But we didn't agree to go on any posse. That money—'

'That money's still in the deal,' Malmgren told him. 'There'll be a good long trip back from where we hang them butchers. Charlie Shields won't be watchin' close.'

'What 'bout Slattery? He'll be along.'

'You let me worry about Slattery. You just get Keelin and Reno to join us. They back me, they'll get their money.'

Nodding, Gil Rachins swung his horse and turned toward the west end. Malmgren rode directly across to the jail hitchrails.

He counted sixteen men, including old Hall

28

and John Davies' young son, a thin, sallow boy of fourteen. All faces watched Dan O'Hearn. The sheriff leaned with both hands flat on the railpost. He'd put on a brand new pair of Levi's, but a stain of blood darkened the fabric where it seeped through the bandage. O'Hearn was washed out, his skin pale, two deep, clear lines at the sides of his mouth. Alf Hager and Fred Johnson, who waited beside him, looked as though they expected he'd keel over any minute.

'And we might be ridin' for a good long while,' the sheriff was saying. He studied old Hall, then shifted to the Davies boy. 'You two drop out,' he told them. Hall's lips parted to answer, but the lawman spoke louder. 'You're too old, Calvin. Billy's too young. Move back so I can swear the rest of the men in.'

Jake Malmgren kneed his gray past the rear line closer to the rail. 'We'll need all the riders we can get, Dan,' he said. 'There's three, four trails they could take once they're through the pass.'

'Calvin and the boy don't come.' O'Hearn's fingers gripped the wood tighter, he bit his lips. 'Move back, you two.'

Reluctantly, the white-haired old man and the boy edged their mounts to the side. Jake Malmgren sat his saddle rigidly. His horse swung its stern, heels chopping. Jake let the animal pivot. The others were just as anxious to get going. Small talk grumbled through the crowd.

'Raise your right hands,' O'Hearn said. He gave the oath slowly. He held the rail tightly, his eyes on their faces while the posse repeated each line. When he finished and let go of the wood, his fingers visibly shook.

'Sheriff,' Slattery said behind him, 'that leg's bleeding again. You should rest.'

'I know what I should do!' The lawman took one step, then another, toward his horse. 'Alf, Fred, help me up.'

Hager and the gunsmith held the sheriff's elbows. O'Hearn raised his good leg to slip the boot into the stirrup, but he didn't have the strength. Two or three of the posse had turned their mounts into the roadway to get started. The others sat quietly, watching the lawman make a second attempt to mount. O'Hearn dropped his foot. His shoulders trembled. He would have fallen if Hager and Johnson weren't supporting his weight.

'C'mon,' a voice in the middle of the group said. 'We've lost enough time. They'll be in Idaho by the time we get started.'

The low grumble grew louder. More of the men pulled their horses away from the railing into the middle of the street.

'We can't wait any longer,' Jake Malmgren said. 'Dan, what you say?'

O'Hearn shook his head. The stain of blood ran from the middle of his thigh to his knee. 'Wait. I'll be all right.'

30

Slattery stepped in next to the lawman. 'That bandage needs changing, Sheriff. You wouldn't make the pass.'

'C'mon, O'Hearn!' Malmgren called. He glanced around at the faces, all set and angry and impatient. O'Hearn moved toward his horse again, slowly, awkwardly.

Slattery said, 'He can't ride like this. Can't you see that?'

'He's got to ride.' Jake Malmgren led his gray back. The animal, feeling the mood of the men, wheeled its stern, switched its tail. 'Who else we got to lead? Hager?'

That brought muffled laughter. More irritated remarks went through the posse. The air was changing fast. Where it had been mostly sunlight, now the clouds had reached the southwestern peaks, hiding the huge red disk. Small hazy beams of sun showed through the breaks, shining for moments on the riders and horses, making the rifles and carbines and metal parts of harnesses glitter. Then the shadows set in again, accompanied by a cool wind that flapped their clothing and blew the horses' tails and manes like plumes. Malmgren stared toward the west. 'You decide, O'Hearn. Either you lead, or I do.'

Charlie Shields, riding in from Cross Street, pulled up alongside Jake Malmgren. His wounded shoulder was hidden by his stiff cowhide coat. He favored his left arm, shifting his weight onto his right side. 'Jake's right,

31

Dan,' he called. 'Either you lead, or one of us will.'

'Give him time to change the bandage,' Alf Hager asked. 'He'll go.'

'There ain't time,' said Malmgren. His gaze ran across the circle of faces; he saw the men were with him. 'I'll handle this till you catch up. You catch up, Dan.'

O'Hearn had strength enough only to shake his head. Slattery said, 'Wait until the sheriff's inside. The deputy can lead.'

'The deputy, hell!' Malmgren shouted. The men around him agreed. They didn't laugh or smirk this time. They simply nodded and watched O'Hearn and Malmgren. Their eyes narrowed, partly in irritation, partly because of the change of the weather.

Malmgren said, 'You swore us in, Dan. I'll have that Frenchie before you catch up.' He jerked hard on the reins to swing his gray into the middle of the street.

Alf Hager and Fred Johnson had started to help O'Hearn step up onto the walk. Slattery moved closer to the hitchrail. 'Malmgren, you haven't the authority to take that man. The law—'

'The law better catch up fast!' Jake Malmgren said. He paused with his boots poised to drive the spurs into his mount's sides. 'You wait for O'Hearn! You be with him when he's ready!'

He didn't stay for an answer. The rowels

32

kicked back and the roan broke into a fast gallop. Shields and five riders, then a sixth and seventh, followed Malmgren.

Slattery hesitated at the rail, knowing it would be useless to try to stop them. Just as hopeless as it would be to stop a lynching once they had the Frenchman, LeDuc. He looked at the men who'd remained, as anxious as their horses to get started. 'Just wait here,' he told them. 'Just wait.'

'We want to go,' a rider said. 'We want the law with us.' Others echoed the statement.

'You'll have the law with you,' Slattery told them. He turned and crossed the walk into the jail office. The men waited.

CHAPTER THREE

Hager and Johnson had lain Dan O'Hearn on the bunk of the first cell. The deputy was bent over the sheriff, unbuckling his belt so he could change the bandage on the wound that stained the entire thigh and knee of the Levi's. O'Hearn's eyes were open, but he'd lost so much blood he didn't have the strength he'd need. He tried to sit by leaning his weight on his elbows. Only his head raised. He strained the entire length of his heavy body. He bit his lips together until they met in a pale, thin line, then he dropped down again on the white pillow.

'How many of them left?' the sheriff asked Slattery.

'Eight in all. Sheriff, they'll lynch LeDuc.' He looked at Alf Hager. 'You're the only other lawman. You'll have to get ready fast.'

Hager gulped. He put his hand to his chin as though he'd been struck in the face. He seemed smaller than he actually was, his slender face suddenly as pale as O'Hearn's. The narrowness of his cheeks and nose were emphasized by the long widow's peak in the middle of his brow. 'Not me,' he said. 'I can't go.'

'You have to. The sheriff wouldn't reach the river. Those men haven't proof LeDuc was hidden in those trees. They'll string him up anyway.' He watched the deputy's bony head move from side to side. 'There's a girl out there, too. Malmgren won't stop with the father.'

'No, I'm not the one.' Hager stared down at O'Hearn. 'He'll bleed to death if the wound isn't fixed. I have to bandage it.'

'Johnson can handle that,' Slattery said looking at the gunsmith. 'The main part of the posse's waiting. They want the law with them, but if you hold them up too long they'll follow Malmgren.'

The deputy's head shook again. 'I've never handled men like that. I've never used a gun.' His eyes moved to O'Hearn. 'Tell him, Dan.'

O'Hearn's voice was as weak as Hager's. 'You go. Get a coat on, Alf.'

Alf Hager faltered. 'Dan?'

34

'Go ahead. Hold them down. If LeDuc wasn't there—'

'Dan, Slattery's sworn in,' Hager offered. 'He can handle the men.'

'Slattery'll back you,' O'Hearn said. 'You'll have to control the posse. Go 'head, get your coat. Move, Alf.'

Hager straightened, slowly. Without a word he walked into the stone cell corridor. Slattery took a step after him. He halted when O'Hearn spoke his name. He moved back to the cot, looked down at the sheriff.

'It'll be up to you,' O'Hearn told him. 'Malmgren'll want blood. You make Alf hold them to the law.'

Slattery nodded, then he hurried from the cell and into the sheriff's office.

*　　　*　　　*

Jake Malmgren did want blood. He'd traveled half a mile from town, holding his horse in the river brush past the spot where Robby had been killed. His brother would be alive now if it wasn't for this stinking Hole. He didn't know why or how, but he and Robby hadn't been able to keep up the ranch after their father had died. He wondered how the old man had eked out a living all those years anyway. The soil was so poor, so rocky and sandy. Not rich and lush like Shields' spread or the meadows they now passed. He'd hoped to give the kid a

35

chance by getting the twelve thousand Slattery had brought in for the cattle. He and Robby could've made a new life somewhere. They could've bought more cows in Idaho with the money and driven them into Slattery's valley in Montana. They could've started over again there. Could've ... could've ... it was all gone now, dead, killed with the bullets that had chopped the poor kid down. But he'd get blood, he'd get the ones who did it.

He had the right men with him. Shields wanted his money and would go along with anything. The rest, despite the fact O'Hearn wasn't in charge, would cut down or string up every last one of the holdup gang. Malmgren looked around. No one talked. They just rode, their hard-boned, roughened faces set and determined to handle and finish anything that came. Most had put on reefers or cowhide coats when they'd struck the open. The wind blew down more like winter than spring, making the men keep their faces turned away from the cold breeze that bent and ruffled the grass. Even the cattle felt the storm. They weren't feeding but moved restlessly in small bunches, their branded rumps to the western cloud-hidden peaks. There were no riders in sight as far behind as Jake could see. The rest of the posse would be held up until O'Hearn was in shape. If he couldn't lead, Hager was the only other authorized lawman who could. That would be something....

The three riders who broke from the brush ahead interrupted Malmgren's thoughts. Gil Rachins appeared first, then Bud Keelin and Reno Wells. Rachin's stubbled jaw turned toward the others for an instant. As soon as he'd spoken to them, his long body straightened in the stirrups to stop his mount. All wore faded work shirts and battered jeans. Keelin, stubbier than Rachins, had on a black flat Spanish hat and two sixguns. Wells, as tall as Rachins, but thinner, watched with his sharp eyes partially hidden by his sombrero. He also wore two sixguns, low-slung and thonged down to his thighs.

'Jake! Jake, hey!' Rachins called before the line of horsemen reached them. 'You said that LeDuc was one of them! He's gettin' ready to leave the Hole!'

'Where? You saw him?'

'At his shack,' Keelin answered. 'Him and that girl of his are fixin' his wagon. He's leavin' all right.'

The riders behind Malmgren pulled in close to listen. They jockeyed into a tight circle, their faces held out of the wind to hear better. One or two swore. Rachins raised his voice for the men at the rear. 'Lucky stayed to watch. I figured you'd want to know, Jake, in case they started.'

'I know, all right.' Malmgren cursed as he spurred his gray. He wanted to let the horse run hard, yet he didn't dare chance going out into the open and let the Frenchie see they were

37

coming. He rode at a lope, slowing to cross the dirt road that cut the Hole from north to south. Eleven minutes later he could see the spot where the creek wound south. A thick growth of timber and brush blocked a good view of the Frenchie's shack. The willows, aspens and alders, and here and there a big bare cottonwood, gave the same cover to his own approach. Lucky Voss stood from where he'd lain under a willow and ran back toward the riders, waving both arms at Malmgren.

'Keep it down,' he warned. 'Keep the noise down.'

'They still there?' asked Malmgren.

'Yeah. Both Frenchie and the girl.' His calm, handsome face studied the others. He rubbed one hand along his thick black sideburns which curled from under his hat to the lower lobes of his ears. 'They're not bother'n with the buckboard. Frenchie's saddlin' the horse.'

Malmgren jerked his Spencer carbine clear of its scarred leather boot. He swung down from the saddle. 'They damnwell won't get far.'

Charlie Shields had stopped his horse alongside Malmgren's. 'What about the rest of them, Jake? There were four more.'

'We'll get them. All of them.' Crouching low, he pushed into the brush. Shields stayed a stride behind him. At the edge of the meadow both sprawled flat. The buckboard, still tilted on its bad wheel, waited near the front door of a small tarpaper shack. LeDuc's horse, saddled, was between the front door and the wagon. It was a clean shot, across open sandy ground. Malmgren pumped the rifle while he braced himself on his elbows.

'They'll come out,' he said tightly. 'I'll get him.'

'Don't shoot him,' said Shields. 'If the others are inside, they'll ride out the back.'

'There's no one else but the Frenchman and his girl,' Lucky Voss told them. 'I been watchin' long enough to know. You c'n get him, Jake.'

Malmgren held the wooden stock hard against his shoulder. Shields reached out and pushed down the long carbine barrel. 'No, Jake. Wait. There's a way.'

Malmgren cursed. 'Look, Shields. Robby was my brother. Just because he worked for you, you don't boss me. I want that Frenchie.'

LeDuc's dark-haired daughter had stepped from the doorway. She had changed her dress for a blue blouse and jeans. She dropped a sheepskin coat across the saddle horn and turned toward the shack again. Before she reached the door her father came outside. They stood close together, talking, both totally unaware of the hidden men. Malmgren began to bring up the iron barrel.

'Like a clay pigeon,' he muttered.

'No, I said.' Shields shoved the carbine down. 'Kill him and we won't learn a thing

39

about the rest of the gang.' He crouched on one knee, motioned to the men who'd grouped behind them. 'Circle out on both sides. We'll get them as soon as they ride off.'

'We'll get them now. Right now,' Malmgren snapped. He'd rolled away from Shields, aimed the carbine. The bang of the weapon came like an explosion in the quiet of the meadows. 'Dammit, I knew I could get him.'

Eduard LeDuc went down. His daughter bent over him, her stare switching from her father to the woods. LeDuc pushed himself onto one elbow and shouted something to her. She reached up alongside the horse's saddle and took a rifle from its boot while her father crawled into the shack. She fired twice haphazardly toward the trees. The bullets went high, snapping branches while they zinged harmlessly into the far flat, but it was enough to make every man dive for cover.

Shields, swearing, grabbed the stock of Malmgren's weapon. Malmgren jerked it away, making the rancher flinch at the pain which shot along his wounded arm.

'You damned fool, Malmgren. We needed LeDuc. Now we'll have to fight him.'

'We'll get him,' Malmgren snarled. 'I'll get him, don't you worry. We'll get the girl. We'll know where the rest went.' He peered towards the shack. The door was shut. The long black barrel of a rifle jutted out the window. It kicked upward as a bullet banged toward the brush.

40

'Move out,' Malmgren shouted to the men who'd followed him. He pressed the stock to his shoulder, aimed, and squeezed the trigger. The wagon horse went down. The animal kicked once, twice, then lay still.

'They ain't goin' anyplace!' Malmgren shouted. 'We'll split up and go in from all sides! Rachins, you circle 'round to the back and set fire to the shack!' He straightened, stared at the listeners, some of them already moving to either side. 'They'll come out quick enough! We'll get them! Both of them!'

* * *

'Shooting,' Tom Slattery said to Alf Hager. 'You hear it?'

The deputy's thin, sensitive mouth curled downward at the corners while he listened. He didn't answer. The remainder of the posse, strung out behind the two lead riders, bunched up as Slattery slowed his black beside the deputy's pinto mare. The horses crowded in too close, the two or three in nearest sidling out, hammering and blowing. 'I hear it,' one of the men said. 'So do I,' agreed another. Slattery watched the deputy. 'There. Ahead,' he told him. 'Where the creek turns south.'

Hager nodded but didn't answer.

'Well, tell them to move,' Slattery said softly. 'Move yourself.'

The deputy nodded vigorously. 'Go in

41

there,' he said, not quite loud enough for all to hear. He spurred his mare, galloped off alongside Slattery's gelding.

Some of the horses wheeled or turned while their riders, who hadn't caught the order, hesitated. Hump bumped rump and spurs caught on trousers. Slattery heard shouts and curses the men snapped at each other. He'd been aware of the men's dissatisfaction when the deputy had left the jail and the posse had seen who'd lead them. Now, the remarks were more bitter, angrier. It was partly because they realized the skinny lawman's weakness, partly because of the feel of the weather. Far to the west the mountains were dark and shadowy under the cloud cover. The cliffs, spotted with pine and checkered with huge sections of lingering snow, looked higher and closer than they actually were. Bad enough to be out in this weather led by someone who didn't know his business. And now gunfire coming so fast....

Slattery saw the horses, eight of them, tied at the outer fringes of the aspens, willows, and alders. He slipped his Winchester from its boot and motioned to Hager. 'They're in the brush. Ahead there. Shields, Malmgren, and another man.'

Malmgren's carbine slammed while Slattery and Hager dismounted and moved into the trees. The Frenchman's home was about eighty sandy, sparsely-grassed yards from the river. A rifle banged from the window of the shack.

Another shot came from the doorway. Malmgren looked around at Hager and waved his weapon in the air.

'Frenchie's in there,' he said. 'We're drawin' his fire so's Rachins can torch the place.'

'The girl's in there too.' Shields told them about Malmgren shooting LeDuc, then said, 'I didn't want it like this. He didn't have to shoot.'

'You didn't have a brother cut down by that Frenchie,' Malmgren said. 'I did, and I'll take care of LeDuc my way.' He nodded to Hager. 'Circle your posse out, Alf. I don't want him alive after he comes through that door.'

Alf Hager hesitated. He seemed smaller and more timid standing between Slattery and Malmgren. Slattery said, 'There's no value in killing him. You aren't even certain he was in that holdup.'

'I am certain.' Malmgren stared Hager down. 'You gonna circle them? Rachins is 'bout ready.'

Hager gazed at the shack, then at Malmgren. 'It might be better if we took LeDuc alive. He can give—'

Malmgren cut him off. 'He'll give us nothing we don't already know. We got tracks to follow for the rest. They go right by here to the pass.'

'But—' Hager began.

'But nothin'. We gotta clean them out 'fore that rain hits and washes out the tracks.' He turned his back on the lawman, crouched

43

down, and fired once, then again at the shack.

Two shots answered the carbine. The posse members, cursing and complaining from fright, scrambled for the cover of the trees and brush. Slattery heard two loud slugs whine over his head and out across the flat. He watched Alf Hager.

'You're the deputy,' he told the lawman. 'You decide.'

Hager had ducked behind a thick cottonwood trunk. His fingers trembled while they held the lever of the Winchester Dan O'Hearn had made him take along.

'Well, decide,' Slattery said sharply. 'Two dead people aren't going to do you any good.'

Hager said, 'We've got to get them out. All I want is to arrest them.'

'We'll get them,' Malmgren spat. He triggered off another bullet, pumped the carbine, and fired again.

Slattery left Hager and went over to Malmgren. 'That's enough,' he said. 'Hold fire.'

'What? I'm makin' it so there'll be a fire.' He grinned, then began to laugh as he aimed the carbine.

'Hold it, I said.' Slattery pushed the long barrel aside. He stepped through the brush. He held his Winchester out clear of his body and cupped his left hand at his mouth.

'LeDuc! Hey, LeDuc!' he shouted. 'Hold your fire! I'm coming in there! Either you hold

44

fire or you'll be burned out!'

He was in the open now. The noises behind him had quieted instantly. There was no other sound in the woods or flat. Slattery let the Winchester slip from his fingers. The soft thud of it striking the sand sounded to him like an explosion.

'Don't shoot, LeDuc. Hold your fire. I'm coming in there to talk.'

CHAPTER FOUR

Behind Slattery Jake Malmgren cursed obscenely. 'Down! Get down, you damned fool! They'll kill you!'

Slattery kept walking, slowly. 'Crazy!' he heard someone say from the brush on his right. Other loud, dumbfounded remarks were made, but he paid them no attention. A man who'd been crawling toward the small building now stood fifty yards to the rear of the shack. He decided to run for it while the Frenchman and his daughter were concentrating on Slattery. Slattery raised his hands higher. 'There are twenty-five men out here, LeDuc,' he called. 'If you don't give up, you'll be burned out. You and your daughter. Throw down your guns and come out. The law will see you're treated fair.'

He was sixty feet from the shack, fifty . . . No

45

movement at either the window or doorway, or sound from the woods. The runner was closer to the building than Slattery was and would reach it first.

'Make up your mind, LeDuc!' Slattery yelled. 'Quick, or you'll be burned out! You want a chance? Make it fast!'

Slowly, the door opened inward. A long-barreled rifle was thrown out onto the sand. A sixgun followed, landing inches from the first weapon. LeDuc's daughter stepped through the doorway into the open. She stood tense and straight, her shoulders held rigidly. She looked directly at Slattery. 'Papa is shot bad,' she called. 'He's bleeding very much.'

'Tell him to come out,' Slattery said.

'He's hurt very badly.' Her deep-set dark eyes flicked to the trees behind Slattery, to the dead horse, then returned to Slattery. She heard the man behind the shack yet she didn't turn toward the clomping of his boots. Her features, dark under the cloudy sky, showed nothing. She backstepped through the doorway, then reappeared immediately carrying a homemade pine chair. Her father, almost doubled over, his left hand pressed along the side of his checkered shirt, was a step behind her. Blood seeped through his rigid fingers and drenched the top of his trousers.

LeDuc sat in the chair, his daughter stood in front of him. 'He is badly wounded,' she said. 'We have no more guns inside. I must tear a

46

towel to use as a bandage.'

The man who'd run from the woods came past the shack. With his Colt he motioned the girl away from her wounded father. 'Stand clear,' he ordered. 'I'll handle him.'

'No. We were promised no harm.' Her eyes watched Slattery.

'I'll bet.' The Colt centered on her. The man's eyes looked the girl up and down, deliberately, insolently, from her legs to the thick black hair that hung over the shoulders of her blouse. 'You're a good one, halfbreed. Damned if you wouldn't make—'

'Go on in and get the towels,' Slattery told the woman.

The sixgun remained leveled at her. 'Look, puncher—' Rachins warned Slattery.

'Go in and get the towels,' Slattery repeated. 'She was promised, mister,' he told Rachins. Both of his hands were at his sides. His right came up and poised above the butt of the .44 Colt that jutted from his waistband. 'Go ahead, girl.'

She turned. Rachins leveled his sixgun and muttered to himself. But he didn't shoot. He stared beyond Slattery to the men who circled in from the river brush. 'What you pullin', Slattery?'

'They have our word. Don't try touching her. Either of them.'

Jake Malmgren's loud gruff voice came from behind him. 'What you waitin' for,

47

Rachins! You got him!'

Slattery gave Rachins no time to answer. 'He isn't touching this man. Or the girl. No one is.'

'The hell you say!' Malmgren's face was white with anger. He glared down at the Frenchman. LeDuc, doubled over to control his pain and bleeding, said nothing. Alf Hager had stopped to pick up the rifle and revolver. A few of the posse had gone back for the horses. The rest came out of the trees, silent and watchful while they moved in. Charlie Shields stepped in alongside Malmgren, his face angry and flushed from the hurried walk. Malmgren brandished his Winchester. 'He's goin' to swing for killin' Robby! He damnwell is!'

'It has to be done right, though,' Alf Hager said. He stepped past Shields, closer to the wounded man. LeDuc's daughter came out of the house with two worn towels, so frayed they tore easily. She knelt in front of her father and gripped his fingers to move them from the wound. 'You had no right shooting him,' she said. 'He's done nothing to any of you.'

LeDuc groaned and said in a low voice. 'Do not beg, Marie. We do not beg.'

'Beg!' Malmgren snapped. He eyed Rachins and Keelin as they went into the shack, then lowered his gaze to LeDuc. 'Won't do you no good to beg, squawman! You killed my brother with that shootin' you did! Beggin' ain't gonna help you!'

Marie LeDuc's face turned upward to the

men. 'Shooting? My father did no shooting?'

Jake Malmgren swore. 'Don't try to cover him! You know why he was shot! You know what he did!'

Marie's hands unbuttoned her father's shirt, but her eyes moved to Charles Shields and she watched him while she spoke. 'I know why you would come. We knew we were not wanted here.'

Shields looked surprised. He touched his own shoulder and traced the line of the bandage below his coat. 'I was hit, too. Bad enough they got my money. He had to make certain he shot me, too.'

The girl watched the rancher for another moment, contempt clear in her expression. 'My father shot no one,' she said quietly. She had the wound exposed. The entire rib area was bleeding from a two-inch long bullet gash below the armpit. Her father grimaced as she pressed along the bone.

Alf Hager said, 'It'll go easier with you, LeDuc, if you tell us where the others went. And who they were.'

LeDuc's bearded face remained calm. 'What is this?' he questioned. 'I shot no one. I know of no others.'

'Come on, you,' Shields said. 'Don't play-act. You didn't cry innocence when we took you. You'll save yourself grief, mister. You'll save her.'

'I know why you came,' the Frenchman

49

answered, his voice tighter. Pain tightened his eyes and mouth, cutting deep lines down into his black beard. 'You could not have my daughter. You saw I was taking her away.'

'Hey! Look at this we found!' Rachins and Keelin hurried from the shack. The tall cattlehand held a small brown canvas bag. He held it by the top so the printing on the front was easy to read: CODY NATIONAL BANK. He loosened the drawstring and showed the money inside. 'Look at this. Greenbacks, more than two hundred dollars here. There's silver dollars in the bottom and more change.'

'String him up!' a man shouted. Other voices joined in, 'String him up! String him up!' A few of the posse members waved coiled ropes above their heads. Malmgren stepped closer to the chair. He reached out to pull the girl to her feet and away from her father. Men pressed forward together, swearing and shouting.

Slattery grabbed Malmgren's arm. He swung around, putting his back to the girl and her father. 'This isn't going to be a lynching.'

'You saw the moneybag!' Malmgren said. 'You brought that money from the Cody bank yourself!'

Slattery's hand was on the butt of his Colt. 'You don't lynch him.' He called to Hager. 'You're the law. Back it, man.'

Hager stuttered and Malmgren shouted, 'My brother was shot down without a chance,

50

Alf! I say we stretch his neck! Now!'

'Hager, you hold them down.' The men crowded around Slattery, whose hand was still poised to draw. He saw a rope swing wildly in the air over the tops of the hats, rifles and carbines aimed at him. 'Hold them, Sheriff.'

Hager backed in beside Slattery. 'This is the wrong way! The wrong way!' He shook his head. 'If he's guilty, he'll hang. But after a trial.'

'Hell with a trial! They murdered poor Robby!'

'That's right, Alf! You see the money! It's from the Cody bank! It's what Slattery brought in!'

'My father got that money by himself,' Marie told them. She'd straightened and was standing in front of her father as though her slim body could protect him. 'He saved that money! He saved every cent of it!'

'She's lyin',' Charlie Shields said. 'If we're not goin' to hang him, I say we take him back. He was runnin'. You saw he was runnin'.'

'We weren't running! You know why we were leaving!' Marie's contempt for the mob, and for Shields himself, was a lash. 'You wanted me! You asked my father for me and when he said "No," you made a threat. Papa was taking me out of this valley! He was!' She scanned the faces, pleadingly. 'You all saw us start to leave the valley this afternoon!'

'They did,' Slattery said. 'They were on the

51

road.' He motioned to the buckboard. 'You were there, Shields. You too, Malmgren. Most of you men saw them try to leave.'

Talk started, a tense, expectant chatter that began to calm the hate and violence. Malmgren watched the posse. Rachins and Keelin had edged in near him. LeDuc's daughter stood rigidly beside Slattery, her breath held tight. The Frenchman just stared downward. He'd lost so much blood he wouldn't last long. The talk quieted almost as quickly as it had flared. Only the chopping of the horses and whistle of the cold wind sounded.

'LeDuc don't hang, not yet,' Malmgren said. 'But he comes along with us. We're chasin' the rest of that gang. He'll be with us when we get them.'

Marie LeDuc shook her head. 'He's lost too much strength.'

'He comes with us!' Malmgren repeated. 'Hager, either he swings now or he comes along!' He touched Rachins' arm. 'You'll ride double with him!' He hadn't moved his eyes from the deputy. 'Either that or we have it out here!'

'He'll come, Jake.' Alf Hager's voice was low. He looked at the girl. 'You'll take care of him. Take my horse, the both of you together. I'll ride with Rachins.'

Malmgren and Shields both opened their mouths to complain. Slattery said, 'That's

52

what the deputy wants, that's what we do. Hager's the law!'

Shields spoke loudly, glaring at the girl and her father. 'I don't like their lyin' about me. They come, they ride in front so they won't try getting away.'

'They won't have a chance to try anything,' said Slattery. 'There are enough men to stop them.'

'There are,' Jake Malmgren said. He let his voice rise so the men at the very rear could hear. His eyes were half-closed, watching carefully while he studied Slattery, questioning him. 'You been makin' damned sure he ain't lynched,' he added with an edge of hate. 'You made sure the stage stopped up on that switchback, too. I figure that's how LeDuc got a good look at just exactly how the money was bein' brought in.'

Now his stare rose to Rachins, Hager, and Keelin. 'That holdup was set up smart. Damn smart, Slattery. Don't you try hidin' off. Don't you try it.'

CHAPTER FIVE

Marie LeDuc kept her head bent, her attention on her father's side while she tied the bandage tightly.

Slattery said, 'Here, I'll help him stand.'

53

The dark-haired girl looked up. Her face was worried. She shook her head. 'You've done enough,' she said. 'We'll take care of ourselves.'

'That's all right. I'll give you a hand getting him onto the horse. You too.'

'No. I'll do it alone. Let me do it alone.'

Jake Malmgren had walked to the horses. He'd mounted with most of the posse and now he turned his roan toward the shack. 'Hurry up, you! Don't try holdin' us here any longer.'

Marie's lovely dark face lost its last trace of warmth. She glanced at Malmgren, and Shields beside him, her eyes cold, inscrutable. 'In a minute. We're ready.' Her head bent low, she took her father's left elbow. 'Easy, Papa. Move slow. Do not open the wound.'

Slattery picked up the sheepskin that Marie had draped across the saddle of the horse that now lay dead. 'He'll need this. Have you got a coat inside?'

'I'll get it,' she said. 'Please, stay by yourself. It is bad enough they suspect us. Do not be a part of it.' She did not wait for his answer. Her father was standing, supporting himself alone. 'I'll bring my coat, Papa,' she told him. 'Wait.'

Slattery watched the girl go into the shack. Alf Hager had climbed into the saddle behind Rachins. The men waited in small groups, doing little talking. Their mounts, after so much standing and fidgeting, had become restless and kept straining to start. One or two

54

began to mill and yank, and their riders let them walk along the sandy yard for twenty or thirty feet before turning them back toward the gathering. The clouds overhead were dark and thick. The sky was brighter off toward the Tetons, the greyish cover above the peaks shifting rapidly like a dense stream that could turn clear at any moment. Slattery hoped the storm would miss the valley, then a cold icy drop of wetness touched his face, and he looked down again through the shack doorway.

Marie had come out wearing a thick woolen jacket. She took the sheepskin from Slattery to put over her father's shoulders. Slattery held the collar while LeDuc slid his right arm into the sleeve. Then carefully, the bearded man raised his left arm so he wouldn't open the bullet wound.

A horse whinnied. Others kicked their hoofs and moved off toward the west. Marie shot a glance at Rachins' mount. Alf Hager waved for her to hurry. 'Come on,' the deputy called. 'You're takin' too long.'

Slattery held LeDuc's left side while the wounded man put his boot into the stirrup. LeDuc strained against him and pulled himself up by gripping the horn. He sat slouched forward a bit and leaned on the horn, panting to get the breath he'd lost by his effort.

Slattery reached out to take Marie's elbow. 'I can do it by myself,' the girl said. Her dark,

55

worried eyes watched Malmgren and Shields. Head high, she lifted her foot and slid it into the stirrup.

Slattery didn't move until she was seated behind her father. 'Call if you have trouble,' he told them. 'I'll be close enough.'

'You stay by yourself.' Marie moved one slim hand, lowering it as if she meant to touch him. She did not. She raised the hand high again and circled both arms around her father. 'We'll be all right.'

'I'll be close.'

'No, you've only hurt yourself by helping us.'

Eduard LeDuc looked down at Slattery. 'She's right,' he said nodding at Malmgren and the rest who waited and watched. 'We'll be all right.'

Marie kneed their mount gently. The horse moved forward slowly.

'Come on,' Malmgren yelled. 'We'll be all night getting to the pass if you don't go faster.' With that Marie kicked the mount. The horse's long legs quickened its stride. Walking toward his black gelding, Slattery studied the clouds above the Tetons. Small breaks showed beyond the peaks, and blue sky was visible. Before he was mounted the wind closed the breaks, eliminating the chance that the rain would miss them.

The posse strung out behind the horse which carried Marie and her father. In the silence that had fallen over the men, even the intermittent patter of the sparse rain seemed loud.

*   *   *

Jake Malmgren watched Slattery pull into line two horses behind LeDuc and his daughter. As Slattery passed him, Malmgren looked downward. Wisps of steam rose from each drop that struck the parched dust of the sandy yard. The hate that controlled Jake Malmgren was as real as the small brownish puffs which vanished with the wind. Only the hate didn't vanish. It rode with him, was in the flick of his wrists that angled his roan into line. He'd wanted to leave the Frenchman hung from a tree, but he hadn't been able to control the men. Too many of them backed what Slattery had used as the law, that sniveling half-excuse for a lawman who held on for dear life to Rachins at the head of the posse. Jake counted twenty-four riders. Too many to have his way. LeDuc would probably die from loss of blood before they crossed the divide if they had to keep going that long, but the thought didn't satisfy Jake Malmgren. There were plenty of trees and rocks jutting out along the pass that could be hooked with a lariat. They'd hold good enough to support the noose he'd put around LeDuc's neck.

Twenty-four men were too many to swing onto his side. He'd have to get rid of Slattery.

Once they caught up with the rest of the holdup gang, there was still the money to be taken. He wasn't losing Robby like that, and the money too. Rachins and the other three hadn't come along for the chase. On the ride back, they'd want to grab the money.

Malmgren slowed his roan. Shields, at the very tail of the line, dragged behind the others. He sat his saddle on his right side, favoring the bullet wound. He'd wanted to play the halfbreed, Jake thought, understanding why Shields had had Slattery bring the cattle payment in as cash. Not that he blamed Shields. The girl was really something, the way she filled those jeans and the blue blouse. Young like that. He'd seen how Rachins had looked at her too.

Shields' stare was guarded as Malmgren fell in alongside him.

'You sure keep your business to yourself, Charlie,' Malmgren said. ''Specially that business back there.'

'Now see here,' Shields began. 'I don't think people are going to believe—'

'People'll believe what they're told. Tell them often enough, they will.' Shields meant to interrupt, but Jake wouldn't let him. 'All right, all right,' he went on. 'You got your own angle, but I've got mine in this. Robby was killed. I know what I want.'

'Jake. I don't talk my business over with you.'

58

Malmgren laughed at the rancher. 'You damned old fool. You think because Rob and me went poor, you're better'n us. You figure because the kid had to take that job for you, we'd buckled under. Well, I'll tell you we haven't. I'm goin' to build up again. And I'll either be with you or against you. You think I'll let you wantin' to play 'round with that squaw die out. I won't, Charlie. I'd almost be willin' to let LeDuc make it back to town and really ruin that fine name of yours, but I'll tell you. You want LeDuc shot, and that girl. I want the same thing.' He waved one hand at the men and horses ahead of them. 'Only we aren't goin' to get what we want, either of us, as long as Slattery has that gang to work on. I want the odds evened.'

'This posse isn't turnin' back. You know that.'

'I know that. Damn well, I know it. I know neither of us is goin' to get what he wants if we don't break up this posse.' He watched Shields carefully. 'You willin' to go along with any idea I have for that?'

Shields nodded slowly. 'I'm not breaking the law. Hager's not the man we need, but I'm not takin' over from him.'

'You won't have to. Just be ready to go along with me when the time comes.' Malmgren dug his spurs into his gelding. The mountains were still three to four miles west. The few small foothills were bare of timber, so

59

the men they hunted wouldn't have used them to hide. Either they went through Beaver Pass or cut off toward the south and headed for the eastern pass. That was Jake Malmgren's one hope. He'd have to wait until he reached the foothills before he knew.

They were opposite the last ranchhouse at the end of the valley. Heck Gore's sprawling white home and barn were visible half a mile behind the trees that lined the roadway. Closer to the hills the hardpack gradually thinned down to a rough rocky lane that ran through the meadows. Here and there deep ruts had been left by wagons. The new grass had sprung up in spots where water from the spring flood had gathered like small lakes in the trail. Malmgren, taking his time, caught up with Rachins, Keelin, and Voss while their horses plodded through one of the muddy sections.

'Take your time,' Malmgren told the three riders. 'Move up right between Slattery and the LeDucs. Stay there till I tell you what to do.'

Nodding, Voss brushed one hand along his black sideburns. He kept the hand over his mouth so anyone who tried to listen would only hear the click of the hoofs in the mud. 'What about the money, Jake? We can't take it from the law.'

'I don't like it either,' Keelin said. 'Me and Lucky don't cotton to crossin' this gang.'

'We won't have to. Not if we get what I want. Rachins, you be between them two horses.

60

And be ready. Check your carbine. You'll be hitting Slattery.'

'Slattery?'

Jake Malmgren flicked his wrist to slow his gelding. 'Either you get him, or there's no money to be had. You see that.' He dropped behind the sorrel, slowed the gelding's step to allow Shields to catch up. He wiped drops of the thickening rain from his face. He needed two things now: the storm to really blow down in full fury, and a good reason to split the posse. He didn't worry about the weather. There were traces of blue sky every now and then above the peaks, but the wind would hold. Slattery was no problem either. Gil Rachins would be right where he couldn't miss. Even in the dark. Jake Malmgren wasn't worried at all.

CHAPTER SIX

The storm did not hit. Except for the few icy drops which fell in the first half hour after leaving LeDuc's, Slattery felt no rain. At intervals he could see streaks of blue, gradually giving way to the hazy gray of dusk, beyond the cleft in the mountain where the pass opened up between two granite walls. The thick black clouds directly above the valley shifted and moved with the bitter cold wind, promising to break one minute, then closing up and threatening rain the next. Slattery watched Marie LeDuc and her father. He was ready to help, but neither the girl nor the wounded man showed any need for it. They rode at the same jog as the posse, slowing their mount like the others once they struck the muddier, softer section of roadway close to the foothills. King, after the long ride from Cody, was tired and edgy. He kept slipping in the soggy turf, coming out of it stiff-legged and wanting to go faster to reach more solid footing.

Dusk was fading to evening when Slattery heard the call from the head of the line. Shields, at the tail end, had spurred his mount. The horse squelch-squelched through the muck, its hoofs kicking up clods of mud, the noise sending the blackbirds and larks fluttering out of the reeds where they had settled to escape the freezing wind.

The posse had bunched up under the nearest foothill, their mounts crowded in alongside each other with the LeDucs in the middle. A trail led off toward the left. It was little more than a rocky lane that skirted the meadows and circled back around the Hole. Rachins and Alf Hager had pulled up close to LeDuc. The deputy's thin face was grayish in the growing darkness. He stared blankly at the Frenchman while Jake Malmgren shouted his question angrily.

'Did they split up here?' he asked the wounded man. When LeDuc gave no answer he added, 'There's tracks leavin' the trail. Was that the plan, to split up here?'

LeDuc's head shook. 'I don't know. I told you I don't know.'

Malmgren muttered an obscenity. Shields had stopped in the rocky lane. He stared down at the tracks. 'How many of them you think cut off, Jake?'

'Three, four horses did. I'm not sure which ones though. They had our horses they took with the money.'

Slattery dismounted and drew King in the bridle behind him. The hoofprints were dug into the turf as far as the spot where the rocks began. He hunkered down, studied the tracks, hearing Malmgren snap at LeDuc, 'You talk, Frenchie. They split up here. How many doubled back?'

Again the wounded man's head shook. 'I wasn't in on the holdup.'

'You were! Dammit, Hager, you make him tell or let me work on him! I'll get him to talk.'

Hager said, 'It'll go easier for you, LeDuc. You better tell us.'

'Better tell us?' Malmgren mimicked the deputy. 'Don't ask him! You either lead this posse, Hager, or let one of us men lead! We've been sworn in! We can lead!'

Hager sputtered nervously, and the men broke into conversation. One or two shouted agreement with Malmgren, but the main body that had backed the deputy at the shack argued

63

against Malmgren's angry words. LeDuc looked down at the mud, not seeming to care what was going on. Marie watched the faces that surrounded them. She saw the hate there, and the wry smile on Rachin's lips. His eyes stayed solely on her, moved from the top of her jacket to her thighs and legs.

'Can't you see he doesn't know about the men who stole the money?' she said. 'Neither of us knows. We tried to leave the valley earlier. We were at the house only because my father wished to be sure the buckboard was safe.'

Talk grumbled among the men, then died as Jake Malmgren spoke. He acted as though he hadn't heard a word the girl had said. 'What are you goin' to do, Hager? We won't learn anythin' unless we can make him talk!' He stepped closer to the deputy, looked directly into Hager's face. 'You either get somethin' done, or I will!'

Hager's fingers rubbed nervously at his mouth. 'Dan O'Hearn wouldn't let anyone harm this man. He—'

'O'Hearn? I don't care about O'Hearn! You're leadin' this posse!' Malmgren gestured wildly toward the pass. 'We gotta split up if we don't find out which way the most of them went! Some'll have to go along the trail anyway! I want to make sure we have enough men with us when we catch up with that gang!'

'If any of them doubled back,' Slattery said, 'it was with the horses they took in the holdup.

I make out only one deep-dug track in the mud.'

Malmgren turned to him. 'You figure that, do you? Well, I saw tracks clear enough before you covered them up leadin' your horse off the trail.' He looked west at the sky darkening even where the clouds had broken high over the peaks. His attention returned to Hager. 'You're handlin' this wrong, I tell you. But you run the show. All I say is we better get someone after the ones who backtrailed 'fore its too dark to see.'

Hager nodded vigorously, glad to have a chance to get off the hook. His voice was strong, confident when he finally spoke.

'You found the trail, Jake. Pick out the men you'll need.'

'Me? No, not me, Deputy. I go through that pass.' He glanced at the riders, scanning them. 'Charlie, you willin' to lead half this gang?'

Charlie Shields nodded.

'Then Charlie'll lead,' Malmgren said. 'He wants his money back, and he'll stick to the trail till he corners the ones who broke off.' He raised his right hand, counted the ten men on his right into a group. 'You'll ride with Charlie. You too, Reno and Voss.'

Slattery asked, 'What if one man led the horses they took off that way? This is what they'd want. To split a posse.'

Malmgren kept his back to Slattery. He faced only Alf Hager. 'I say we have to split.

65

I'm not lettin' Slattery tell me. You decide, Deputy. Do we do it my way or his?'

'Yours,' answered Hager quickly. 'Yes, yours, Jake.' He motioned to the men Malmgren had counted. His voice was louder, surer now that he'd made the decision. 'Stay with Charlie Shields. Whatever Charlie says, goes.' He tightened his grip around Rachins' waist. 'It's gettin' dark. We better move on.'

Malmgren said, 'Alf, we're goin' to need every gun we've got.' He glanced from rider to rider, stopped with his eyes on a young blond man of about twenty. Both Bob Clark and his father, Will, the middle-aged horseman alongside his son, were known as quiet men. They very seldom came to town, but had happened to be in Beaver Hole when the robbery occurred, and Malmgren had helped them get horses at the livery. They were both well-liked and trusted by everyone in the valley. 'Alf, you climb up behind Bob here. I want Rachins ready so he can fight in case they try bushwackin' us. He'd be slowed by two on a horse.'

Alf Hager didn't argue. While he climbed down and walked to Clark's horse, the other men glanced carefully at one another, all realizing who now ran the posse. One man coughed and looked above them into the pass. Others pivoted their mounts, moving to allow the twelve Malmgren had chosen to fall in behind Charlie Shields.

66

Malmgren turned his back to Alf Hager. 'If they've gone through the east pass, they'll aim to join up with the rest,' he said to Shields. 'You catch up with us, Charlie. We'll leave enough of a trail.'

'Right, Jake.' Shields turned his roan. Jake Malmgren swung up into the saddle and rode ahead with Gil Rachins.

Rachins said, 'I'll stay with you, Jake.'

'You hang behind LeDuc's horse just where you were. When I move, get your gun out and start shootin'. I'll fix it.'

'Jake, I never threw down on a woman.'

'Not the woman. Slattery. You let her horse run past Slattery. Have him between you and them when you shoot.' Malmgren glanced across the shoulder of his heavy leather coat. He lifted his right arm, made a gesture like a cavalry officer directing his troops. 'Gotta move quick now,' he ordered. 'Don't straggle.' He rode toward the mountain looming up in the growing darkness ahead of them.

*   *   *

Marie LeDuc kneed her horse forward. Slattery had stepped into the trail near her, but she paid him no attention. He'd helped them twice since her father had been shot, and he'd only gotten himself deeper and deeper into their trouble. Marie didn't know what would happen. She only knew there was absolutely no

67

chance for escape. The riding they'd done already had weakened her father to the point where he leaned more and more on the horn. She had to hold tighter to keep him in the saddle. They'd move slower once the trail opened up into the pass a quarter of a mile ahead. The rocky mountain road climbed stiffly almost from the start. Their horse, weighted down, had slid and stumbled in the muck, and she feared what a fall could do to the bullet wound. In the dark, with all the rocks that had washed down during the winter, there was even more chance of an accident.

Slattery's voice came from close behind her. 'If you're tired, I'll change with you.'

She spoke without turning her head. 'I'm not tired.'

'Marie, we'll be out all night. Maybe longer.'

'I can hold him. We will be all right.'

'Marie?'

Now she turned her head. The features of her lovely face were barely visible in the thickening night. But her tone was unmistakable. 'Don't try to help us,' she said pleadingly. 'You can't help. You'll just only keep hurting yourself.'

She kicked the horse forward faster. Slattery didn't keep after the girl. He held King at a steady pace with the LeDucs, waiting in case they needed help, ready to give that help.

'He shouldn't be doin' it, Deputy! You should! You're leadin' this posse! No one touches him but you!'

Alf Hager edged past Malmgren to Slattery. The coat was wide open, the wounded man's checkered shirt pulled aside by Slattery's fingers. No blood was visible. Hager's thin hands reached out and gripped the coat. 'I'll fix it,' he said to Slattery. 'I'm in charge. I'll handle the prisoner.'

'Then handle him,' Slattery said flatly. 'You'll have to answer any questions when we get in. You do what you know is right.'

Hager gave no answer. He kept his back to Slattery, his attention on the job of buttoning the coat. Jake Malmgren shook his head at the onlookers, then he walked toward the spot where he'd left his horse.

Hager finished with the buttons. Without a word he moved toward Clark's mount. Slattery stepped in next to him and touched his arm. 'Alf, most of these men will side you all the way. But if you decide the wrong thing, that man and his daughter won't live to get back to Beaver Hole.'

'They'll live,' the thin man answered. 'They're all right. I checked and they're all right.'

'They won't be if they have to keep up like this.'

'They'll be all right. They will.' He suddenly shivered, and Slattery could feel the tremor go

72

The horses climbed the rocky mountain trail with a slow, choppy gait. Slattery dropped back as the pitch steepened, and Rachins took the spot directly behind the LeDucs. Malmgren, Alf Hager and the Clark boy were out of sight in the darkness. Slattery could make out only one rider ahead of the LeDucs. It was Bob's father, and he and his horse were vague shadowy shapes. The temperature dropped as the wind shifted north. The ground at the inner edge of the roadway, muddy from seepage, was already stiffening for the night. The narrows above them looked mile-high. Stars sparkled white in the breaks, and as the clouds shifted, the first trace of the rising moon glistened on the patches of snow above the timberline. The creek which emptied out into the valley amidst the willows, aspens, and alders cut deeper and deeper to the left, making that side of the trail hang on the cliff, the edge becoming sharper and more dangerous the higher they rode.

Moonlight sifted down after the first hour. The strung-out posse grew clearer. Slattery dropped back further. He looked downward, hoping to see the men who'd gone with Shields. Either them, or Augustin Vierra. Gus should have known about the posse since the middle

69

of the afternoon. Slattery wondered what held him up. The sooner they caught the killers, the sooner he'd be able to start the cattle north to Montana. The ranchers who'd trusted their money to him hadn't expected he'd go off like this. The sight of Marie LeDuc with her arms tight around her father made him think of his own woman, Judy Fiske, who waited in Yellowstone City. He couldn't break off and leave. Not with Malmgren like he was. The girl and her father wouldn't stand a chance against the whole gang. Malmgren's hate was too strong. Hager wasn't the man to hold him in control.

Five hundred yards below the summit, the road leveled off for a short stretch. The lead riders slowed, then stopped to breathe their horses. The posse bunched up, keeping close to the inner wall. The rush of the creek was loud, dulling the sound of voices and conversation, so Slattery couldn't hear what was being said when he stopped King. Malmgren, Rachins, and Keelin stood together, Clark and his son with Alf Hager. The others waited in pairs. Those whose coats were not as heavy and thick as Slattery's sheepskin swung their arms across their chests or pounded their fists together to keep warm. No one helped either Marie or her father dismount. The two had reined in flush against the rock wall to keep out of the cutting cold which whipped down from the summit. Slattery dismounted alongside their horse.

'You should stretch your legs,' he said quietly. He offered the woman his hand. 'Here, step off easy.'

Hunched against her father's spine, Marie didn't move. 'I can't leave him alone. He can't hold on alone.'

'I'll hold him. Come on now.'

'No. We're all right.'

Marie stared down at him, her hand touched his. 'Will you open his coat? I'm not sure hi wound hasn't opened.'

Her bearded father mumbled something, th words jumbled and lost under the wail of t wind and rush of the creek. Slattery raised hands to unbutton the sheepskin coat.

'What you doin' there?' Jake Malmg yelled. He hurried toward Slattery. 'D touch him!' Rachins and Keelin were a s behind him. Hager and the rest circled in

Slattery undid the top button, the second. 'He might've started bleeding,' he 'I'm checking.'

Malmgren stopped with his long squa just inches from Slattery's. 'You don't dammit. What do you think this is?'

The third button was undone, the Slattery opened the thick coat. Malmgren turned on Alf Hager. 'Y ri there like that? You watch him do wants like that?'

Hager said weakly, 'He's only ch blood.'

along the deputy's arm. Slattery asked, 'You all right?'

'Yes. Yes, I'm fine. Fine. I'll see they're kept safe. Don't worry. But don't you take anythin' into your own hands. Don't try.'

'I'm not trying, Deputy. I'll back you.'

'Don't try. Don't try then.' He pulled his arm from Slattery's fingers and walked on. 'Mount up. We'll mount up,' he called to the men around him. 'Let's get moving.'

Slattery studied Hager's small, thin figure. He moved as though he were half-drunk. The man was close to cracking, yet there was no step Slattery could take to help him. He could only stay near the LeDucs to help. He turned toward the horse that held the two riders. Marie had already started the animal ahead to follow in line with the posse.

* * *

'Watch out and get ready,' Jake Malmgren said to Rachins. 'Be in place when we reach the top.'

'I'll slow with Gil,' Keelin said. 'Two of us can't miss.'

'You stay here. Right where you've been. Gil'll be spotted to hit Slattery. No one'll think twice 'bout him.' Keelin rode in silence and Jake Malmgren glanced beyond the edge of the cliff. He saw only the rearing, solid shadows of the mountain, black where the forest climbed

73

its side, the patches of snow whitish-gray under the streaks of moonlight. No one would see Rachins take aim.

'Shootin' starts,' he told Keelin. 'You block the ones up front from comin' back too fast. Give Gil time.'

Bud Keelin rode ahead. Malmgren eased his body around in the saddle and glanced at the ghostlike shadow of the horse that held the LeDucs. The pitch was getting steeper at every step. He could feel his roan's shoulders pump as the horse's breathing came in jerks. The narrows thinned to a trail barely wide enough for two horses. The wind buffeted his face and body. The air smelled of snow, and he could smell the acrid odor of smoke, too.

On the summit the wind struck full force. The moonlight brightened and shone down on him. Malmgren held his roan in more. He fought the bitter cold, the wind, and thought only of the space he had, that he had to be careful he didn't push the LeDucs off the edge.

Hugging the wall he heard the clops of the horse's hoofs behind him. LeDuc and his daughter were almost abreast of him.

Malmgren jerked at the gelding's reins, yanking the animal to the left away from the wall. The gelding was too slow. Malmgren dug the spur of his right leg in deep. The gelding screamed into the wail of the wind and swung its rump fast.

Marie LeDuc had seen the trouble

Malmgren was having. She'd started to pull her horse back. Awkward because of her father, she'd succeeded in starting the turn. Then her mount panicked and whirled full around as Malmgren's horse struck it.

Malmgren grabbed the horn, crouched to hold the saddle while he jerked his left boot clear of the stirrup and kicked Marie's horse. The girl tried to stop the swing, but she'd lost control.

Another kick of the boot and the LeDuc horse was running, heading wildly for the cliff edge. The animal sensed the danger and swung left as it charged past Rachins' horse.

Malmgren had both boots in the stirrups. He straightened in the saddle and stood while he stopped his gelding. The LeDucs were ten feet beyond Rachins, their mount galloping hard. Malmgren couldn't see Slattery clearly, but he knew Rachins could. He waited a second longer.

'Stop them!' he screamed loudly. 'They're tryin' to get away! Rachins! Shoot! Shoot them! Cut them down!'

CHAPTER EIGHT

Rachins' left hand strained on the reins while he quieted his mount. His right had dropped to his holstered sixgun the instant he'd heard

75

Malmgren's first yell. He'd swung the horse before the LeDucs' mount had charged past. Now he watched the two shadowy forms move past Slattery, their horse still so close to the cliff edge Rachins thought they might drop off. The moon was half covered by cloud, the pass below the narrows black dark. Rachins waited, his left leg flush with the wall that went straight up, fifty, sixty feet above him. The clomping of the hoofs echoed against the solid stone, above the roar of the creek and whistle of the wind.

Slattery turned to go after the LeDucs, he and his horse a shadowy figure in the hazy light. Rachins, his right arm outstretched, aimed high at the head, his finger on the trigger.

*　　　*　　　*

Slattery slapped hard on King's flank. The LeDucs were so near the edge he was afraid to yell. Yelling could spook their horse even more. He was ten feet behind them, eight.... His left hand was ready to turn the reins around the horn. Both man and horse knew what had to be done. He made the turn, snubbed the thin leather, and crouched forward in the saddle, pressing his stomach against the pommel for support, head bent low, arms reaching....

He heard the bang of a gun, the crack low under the hoof thumps and roar of the water

76

below. He was hit in the right shoulder, the bullet stinging like a whip, and he crouched even lower. A second, then a third shot banged behind him, followed by the zings of slugs above his head, past his ear.

His fingertips almost touched Marie's shoulder. King's long neck drew ahead of the bay horse's tail and rump. 'Toward me!' he shouted. 'In, Marie! Swing toward me!'

No answer. He couldn't see their faces, but he had his hand on the reins. He gripped tight, slammed his right knee into King. 'Over! Over, boy! Over!'

Horses and riders continued along the edge of the precipice another few yards, King turning in slowly, the LeDucs' horse fighting to jerk itself free of Slattery's hold. King edged in and Slattery pulled with him, angling the runaway in, trying to slow and stop him.

They were clear of the cliff. Slattery's left knee slammed King's side. King worked against the other horse. Straining, pulling, Slattery slowed the terrified animal. Marie and her father leaned toward him, pressing against him while the runaway came to a halt.

Hoof thumps pounded behind them. Men shouted and screamed at one another. The LeDucs' mount shied away, lifted its long neck and snorted as Slattery dismounted, his right hand still tight on the reins. The moon slid out from behind the clouds, flooding the summit and narrows in a whitish-gray light.

77

LeDuc hung over the pommel, held tightly by Marie. Slattery reached up to take the wounded man's shoulders.

'He'll bleed more,' Marie said. 'Don't move him. I'll hold him.'

'He could be bleeding now. All that jouncing. I've got him. Lower him easy.'

'No. No. I don't dare.'

'Lower him, Marie. I have to look. Easy now. Easy.'

The galloping horses charged toward them kicking, scraping, and scuffing the trail while Slattery supported LeDuc. Eduard LeDuc groaned and mumbled incoherently. Jake Malmgren shouted a stream of obscenities and jumped from his saddle. 'What you doin'? Leave him be! Put him back on that horse!'

Slattery, straining to lower LeDuc, felt a twitch of pain in his shoulder, and the warm stickiness of blood under his coat, yet he spoke calmly. 'Unhook his foot, Marie. Careful, don't jerk it. Don't let it drop.'

LeDuc's boot came free of the stirrup, and Slattery had him in his arms. He was like a sack of jelly, limp while Slattery lowered him carefully, tenderly, to the stony ground.

The rest of the posse had reached them, Clark and Hager at the rear. Down on one knee, Marie beside him, Slattery began to undo the top of LeDuc's coat. Marie unbuttoned from the bottom.

Malmgren's boots scraped stone and dirt.

78

He grabbed Slattery's shoulder. 'He's all right. He can ride.'

Slattery hit him then. He brought his left up straight in a vicious backhand that smashed Malmgren's face flush along the jawbone. Malmgren went sprawling into Rachins, who stumbled, holding the off-balance man tight until he caught his own footing.

Bob Clark and his father moved forward to stop a fight. Hager stood frozen near his horse, watching Malmgren regain his footing and grab for his gun.

'Don't!' Hager shouted. 'Don't! Don't!'

Most of the posse members jumped aside to clear the space between Malmgren and Slattery. The Clarks held their positions. 'You don't throw down on a man's back,' Will Clark warned. 'You don't try it, Malmgren.'

Jake Malmgren straightened on his heels, the revolver in his hand leveled at Slattery, bent over attending to LeDuc. Marie stared across her shoulder, her face fearful. She looked at Slattery. 'Tom,' she whispered.

'He won't be fool enough,' Slattery said. 'Not with ten witnesses.' He unbuttoned LeDuc's shirt. The seeping blood reflected the moonlight. 'Hold the shirt open. I'll tighten the bandage.'

'Damn you, Slattery!' Malmgren cursed. 'You got no right!'

Slattery kept on working. 'Hold it open, Marie,' he repeated easily. 'This'll stop the flow.'

'You're holdin' us up,' said Malmgren. He shoved the sixgun into its holster, then turned to Alf Hager. 'Deputy, they tried to get away. You saw them. Now he's holdin' us up like this. I say we don't waste one more minute. They used up time runnin' like that.'

'We did not try to get away,' Marie said to Malmgren. 'You—'

Malmgren's shouts bellowed above her words. 'You seen what happened, Deputy.' He scanned the listeners, saw the nods of agreement. 'Gil Rachins was right behind them. If I didn't yell, they might've made it.'

'They were runnin' 'fore I could stop them,' Gil Rachins told the posse. 'Alf, I fired high to stop them. They slowed so Slattery got them.'

Slattery said something to Marie, and the girl began to button her father's shirt. LeDuc lay quietly on the ground, his eyes open, following Slattery's movements. Slowly, Slattery stood.

'You shot low, Rachins,' Slattery said. The hard tightness of his words shifted every man's attention to him.

He walked slowly over to Hager, Rachins and Malmgren. He opened his sheepskin and felt along his right shoulder. He offered his hand, palm up, for the posse to see the streaked blood. 'You fired low enough, mister. Only I'm not sure your aim was that far off.'

'What the hell you sayin'?' Rachins edged

back a step. Malmgren moved to side him and said, 'I yelled for Gil to get them. You got in the way, Slattery. That's your own fault.'

Slattery didn't take his eyes from either man. A long moment of silence fell. The moonlight threw dark shadows onto the three faces. Finally Alf Hager said, 'It was a mistake. It was, Slattery. He was trying to stop them.'

'By drawing on me?' Slattery said. 'When LeDuc was down?'

Alf Hager uttered a low, whimpering sound. 'What are we doin'? What? We're out after killers and we're fightin' each other! I didn't want this! I don't want to waste more time!'

Jake Malmgren's voice had softened. 'We don't either, Deputy. But you see how Slattery's helped them two. They—'

Marie LeDuc cut in. 'That's all he's done. He's only tried to help us. Please,' she pleaded to Hager. 'You are the lawman. If you don't believe my father, don't make Mr Slattery a part of what is happening. He only tried to help.' She stood alone, awkwardly, helplessly, looking down at her father, tears in her eyes. 'He will die if he does not get rest. I couldn't have stopped the horse alone.' She looked from her father to Slattery. 'He only helped him live.'

Hager's thin face was flustered. He bit his lips together, rubbed one bony hand along his mouth. 'I don't know. I don't know.'

Marie gestured hopelessly. 'He must get to

81

where he can rest. The bandage must be changed. Please, he didn't do anything. He did not!'

Bob Clark said, 'There's Macrina's station halfway down the other side. We can make that.'

'Please,' Marie said. 'You are the lawman.'

Alf Hager studied Eduard LeDuc, trying to decide. The bearded man hadn't moved during all the trouble. His eyes were closed. As far as Hager could tell in the semi-darkness, the man might already be dead. The deputy nodded, slowly. 'We'll take him to the station.'

Malmgren said, 'He tried to get away, Hager. You'll have to answer for that when we get back.'

'If he dies, you'll have to answer for that, too,' said Slattery. He nodded to Bob Clark. Both young Clark and his heavy-set father moved forward to help with LeDuc.

Alf Hager didn't speak a word. He stood rigidly, watching Slattery and the others lift the wounded man. He heard Slattery say to Bob Clark, 'We'll put him on your horse with you.' Then Marie LeDuc said, 'On our horse. He's my father. I can hold him. I want to hold him.'

Jake Malmgren made a guttural sound, then spat loudly. 'You catch up, Hager. You're playin' nursemaid, you can damnwell catch up.' He swung around with Rachins. Keelin had edged in behind the pair, and the three stomped off together. Four more of the posse

82

trailed along behind them.

Marie LeDuc had climbed onto her horse. With Bob Clark on her left side, she helped Slattery and Bob's father move her father into the saddle. 'Oh, careful. It's all right. You'll be all right,' she said when her father moaned and began muttering incoherently. 'He's fine now. I have him.'

Slattery looked at Alf Hager standing alone, his stare flicking between LeDuc and the men who'd gone with Malmgren. Will Clark had returned to his own mount. Hager backstepped to Bob's bay, his eyes following the men going onto the summit. 'Hurry up,' he said to Bob Clark. 'Hurry!'

Slattery touched Marie's hands which were tightly clasped around her father's chest. He lifted the reins and hooked them across the saddle horn. 'I'll ride behind you,' he told her. 'Let the horse make its own time.'

She nodded and rode toward the narrows. Slattery walked to King. He patted the black gelding's neck. 'Good boy,' he said quietly. 'Good boy.' He pulled himself aboard, taking a deep breath of the cold, windy air. He'd thought he'd smelled smoke before LeDuc's horse had run. Now, he was certain of it.

* * *

Jake Malmgren also smelled the smoke, just as he'd smelled it when he'd first struck the summit. He gave it no attention. On a night like this every ranchhouse in the territory would have a wood fire blazing, and the smell would naturally be carried along with the wind. Lou Macrina would have his fireplace going. Jake knew Lou as well as any man in the posse. Half the distance down into the next valley the road ran through a clearing. Overland Stage Lines had built a way station there, but they'd abandoned the building three years ago. There was no grass for the horses. The agent had to get his water from either Beaver Hole or Buffalo Hole at the bottom of the steep narrow trail. Too many caves spotted the terrain on this side of the mountain. A man wasn't safe out alone, with the mountain lions, wolves, and occasional bears which were around. That hadn't stopped Lou from taking on the station as a combination home and barroom. He and his wife ran the place with the help of an odd-jobs man, and they catered mainly to the stages that did stop and punchers off the local ranches who wanted to tie one on. Malmgren was thinking of Lou while he rode along. He didn't figure any of the cattlehands would be out tonight. But if one was, he might've seen the riders they were after. Lou, his wife, or Jesse could've seen them go by. Malmgren looked at Rachins, who'd been making excuses since they'd mounted again. Jake was sick and tired of his mouthing.

'Forget it,' Malmgren said. 'There'll be

other chances.'

'But I had him, Jake. He must've ducked lucky. I know I had him.'

'I said there'll be another chance.' Malmgren glanced behind them. The four who'd followed them back in the narrows were strung out single file. Hager and Bob came next, then Will Clark in front of the LeDucs and Slattery. He had Hager on the run, and he knew it. Wetterholm, Gassen, Yeager, and Zino wouldn't be any problem. Just the Clarks to worry about after they'd shut up Slattery. And they would shut him up. Two things Jake Malmgren wanted—to see to it every last one of the men who'd killed Robby died as hard as the kid had, and to finish Slattery before they reached the money. It had cost him so much, he had to have the money.... Malmgren said to Keelin, 'After we leave Lou Macrina's you hang back with Slattery. He'll be watchin' Gil. You'll have a better chance.'

'Jake, I'll drop back now and force him off the trail,' Keelin said. 'He's made enough trouble already.'

'You have ten witnesses. There'll be a Federal Marshal in on this when we get home. You see how Hager is already.'

Keelin's round, jowly face nodded. He answered bluntly. 'We don't have to go back. That cash is what I want. I get my share, I aim to keep ridin'.'

Rachins agreed. Malmgren snapped at

them. 'No, dammit. You know Dan O'Hearn'll be out. We take the money, but we do it so it looks like that gang stashed it. Hager'll—'

'Hager won't stop anything,' Keelin said. 'He can't stop anything.'

'Damn right he can't,' Rachins agreed. 'We corner that gang, there'll be shootin'. We can get behind Slattery and finish him. Hager'll be easier than that.'

'Wait and see,' said Jake Malmgren. He smelled the smoke again, stronger now. They'd at least have time to breathe the horses and get a drink at Lou's. The road below them became steeper, rockier, with a few little washes here and there that they had to watch out for. The moonlight was blocked by the trees on both sides of the trail. Pine needles on stone could be slippery. 'Watch it,' he added. 'A horse breaks a leg, we won't do any catchin'.'

Malmgren pulled ahead of the other two. Gil Rachins looked at Keelin, but the moonlight shaded Keelin's face and he couldn't tell what he was thinking. Rachins was still angry he'd missed Slattery. He agreed with Jake and Keelin about getting Slattery, and he'd go along with what they planned. His agreement with Malmgren ended there, though. Malmgren wanted things set up so he could go back to his one-horse spread and try to build again. Gil Rachins wanted no more part of Beaver Hole. He'd ridden in as a drifter

86

looking for work. He had his chance to build someplace else once he had his cut of the twelve thousand. He didn't care if Hager or every last one of the posse didn't get back to their town. He'd take off. He knew Voss and Reno Wells were for taking off too. He'd talk to them about it once both parts of the posse joined again. Slattery wouldn't be there to stop them. Hager, the others in the posse, even Jake Malmgren, wouldn't be able to stop them.

CHAPTER NINE

Alfred Hager was in no condition to stop anything. He was lost and confused. He'd tried to hide his fear from the others, but they knew. He'd seen it in their faces, heard it in their voices. Slattery ran the posse now. Or Malmgren did. Hager wasn't sure which. He only knew he was caught between them. He wasn't a gunfighter. Dan O'Hearn had handled everything that came up. O'Hearn hadn't wanted to take him on in the first place, but he had because his wife nagged him until he'd agreed to it. O'Hearn had sworn him in as deputy simply because the town council wouldn't pay for a janitor.

Hager let go of Bob Clark's coat, raised both hands to his coat collar and tightened his neck. He was freezing, shivering. The cold ran down into his chest, turned his stomach sour. He felt it all along his back and his arms. In his head he felt it. . . .

The deputy then wrapped both arms around Bob Clark's stomach again and held on. Clark did not say a word. Hager dropped his right hand to try to rub some warmth into his cold leg. His fingers accidentally brushed the sixgun he'd been ordered to take along by Dan O'Hearn. He shuddered, he hated guns. He was scared to death of them. As a boy he'd seen a man shot to death in the middle of Front Street in Miles City, and he'd never forgotten the way the man had twisted and turned while he was dying. He'd even dreamed about it, seeing himself as that man, the pain as vivid as the cold felt now. Hager wasn't only afraid of the men they were chasing. He was scared of Jake Malmgren. Jake was mean. . . . Alf Hager pounded his hand against his leg, hitting the sixgun, beating it. He didn't want to carry it, he didn't want to see it, and he didn't want to be the leader of the posse.

Hager had become aware that the smell of smoke had grown stronger before he saw Malmgren, Rachins, and Keelin suddenly spur their horses into a gallop. They'd reached the break in the pines where the trail opened out into the clearing, and suddenly they were gone from sight.

The four behind them rode hard, also heading into the clearing. Bob Clark kicked his horse forward. Hager stared around at LeDuc and his daughter, and Slattery behind them. They were his chief responsibility, and they couldn't hurt him. But what was ahead, anything ahead could....

The cold icy feeling grew inside Alf Hager the instant the horse moved to where he could see the old stage station.

'Oh, look at that,' Bob Clark breathed.

Hager stayed quiet, fearing what he saw, what he smelled.

The smoke stink was sickening, unmistakably burned horseflesh. Where there had been a low, long, thatched-roofed building, only smoking timbers were visible. The small swaybacked barn and corral behind it smoldered. The first riders had stopped at the house. Malmgren and Rachins had dismounted and were poking through the ruins. The others either sat their saddles rigidly or climbed down to get a better look.

Keelin joined Rachins and they walked around the side of what had been the kitchen and bedroom end of the house. Hager could hear Rachins call across his shoulder, 'Not here. Don't see either of them, or Jesse either.'

'Keep lookin',' Malmgren said. 'They gotta be here.'

Rachins went deeper into the ruins, poking at the blackened wood, causing little spurts of flame to flash up here and there. He stared into the yard. 'They ain't here. I told you, Jake.

89

None of them.'

Jake Malmgren said something Hager couldn't hear clearly. The men who'd remained with the horses glanced from the house to the barn, quietly, angrily, not paying any attention to the deputy or Clark as they drew up. Rachins and Keelin stared back along the trail at the sound of the LeDucs and Slattery coming into the clearing, but they didn't say a word.

Hager studied the stone stoop of the doorway. It looked like Indians had attacked the place, the stink of the dead horses coming from the barn, the thick, choking smoke.

'What happened?' Hager asked the men.

'How in hell do we know?' Meric Wetterholm snapped at him. 'Dammit, Alf, you're in charge. You should take over.'

Hager's mouth tightened and he pulled back in the saddle as though he'd been slapped. The LeDucs stopped alongside him. Slattery dismounted closer to the ruins. 'Will you help Mr LeDuc?' Slattery called to Bob Clark before walking into the ashes.

'Hey! Hey there, Mr Hager!' a voice called from the pines across the roadway.

Slattery's head snapped around with the others. Lew Gassen, standing near the smoldering barn, whirled and leveled his rifle. His deep-set eyes squinted above the bandanna he'd tied over his nose and mouth to keep out the terrible smell.

90

'Don't shoot!' Bob Clark yelled. 'It's Jesse! Don't shoot!'

A boy ran towards them, tall and gangling, with arms that dangled down to his long legs. He was not more than sixteen or seventeen. His white teeth shone bright against his dark skin as he hurried toward Alf Hager.

'Mr Hager! I'm glad you come, Mr Hager!' He was crying and the words jumbled together in his thick Alabama accent. 'You see what they done! See it! Mr O'Hearn? Where's Mr O'Hearn?'

Jake Malmgren said, 'Hager's in charge, Jesse. Control yourself, boy. You control yourself.'

Jesse Gabriel stopped and pointed ahead. 'They shot them!' he said. His eyes shifted from one face to another. Blood was caked on the short kinky hair and down over his right ear to his neck. He wore a light blanket coat which was torn and dirty. He shivered as he stood there staring at the ruins. He waved one arm back across the road. 'They shot Mr and Mrs Macrina too! They jest opened up and shot them!'

Hager said, 'Lou and Martha Macrina?'

'They're over there!' Tears streamed down the Negro boy's bony cheeks, the wetness glistening in the moonlight. 'They'd've been burned! I took them out of the house and put them across there in case they come back! I hid 'cause I thought you could've been with them!'

'Who?' asked Hager. 'Jesse—'

Jake Malmgren cut in. 'You know who, you stupid old woman.' He brushed past the deputy and halted near the boy. 'How many of them were there, Jesse?'

'Five. That's how many I saw.' He stared at Bob and Will Clark while they lowered LeDuc to the ground, then flicked his gaze to the pines beyond the trail. 'I left them out there so they'd be safe. I didn't want them burned.'

'Oh hell,' Gil Rachins said. 'He's too jumpy to tell us anythin'. We move on, Jake. We c'n see what happened.'

Slattery said, 'You were shot, too, Jesse. Calm down now. What happened?'

Unconsciously the boy raised his right hand and pressed it over the caked blood. He flinched at his own touch. 'I was hit. And Mr and Mrs Macrina.' He sobbed. 'They were so good to me. So good to me.'

'Take it slow now, easy,' said Slattery. 'Five men, you say?'

Jesse studied Slattery and seemed to calm. 'I was sweepin' up when they rode in. They asked Mrs Macrina for food and bandages, 'cause one of them was hurt.'

'Hurt?' Slattery asked. The listeners began to talk, and Jake Malmgren shouted, 'Shut up! All of you, shut up!' His tone quieted the chatter, then Slattery asked, 'How bad hurt, Jesse?'

'He must've been hit when Robby fired,' Alf

Hager said. 'Where was he shot?'

The boy shook his head. 'I didn't see him good. Soon as they come in, Mr Macrina, he sent me into the kitchen for steak. I was cuttin' it when Mr Macrina come back and told me one of them was hurt. He got his Colt out of his room. He knew they'd come through the pass, and he told me to get my horse and ride to Beaver Hole and tell Mr O'Hearn.' His eyes moved to Alf Hager. 'I thought Mr O'Hearn'd be out.'

'He ain't,' Malmgren said. 'There's four dead horses in the barn, Jesse. You didn't even saddle one of them.'

Jesse nodded briskly. 'Didn't have time. I got out the back and into the barn. One of them followed me. He opened the door while I was leadin' my horse from the stable. He shot me right there, Mr Malmgren. I don't know what happened. I woke up and the barn was on fire. So was the house. It was still burnin' an hour ago, so they must've stayed a good long time.' He took a deep breath and his thin body quivered. 'Mr and Mrs Macrina were inside. I drug them out. I left them in the woods till I could see to—'

'All right, we know,' Rachins said. He nodded to Malmgren. 'They left only an hour ago, they haven't got too much distance on us.'

Nodding, Malmgren glanced toward LeDuc on the ground. 'Okay, put him into that saddle. We'll get goin'.'

93

Bob Clark said, 'I don't know. He's pretty bad. Alf, he can't take much more.'

'He comes along,' Malmgren said, his face turned to Alf Hager. 'I want him with us.'

Hager said quickly, 'Put him back in the saddle, Bob.' He hesitated when Marie straightened and looked at him. 'He'll die,' she said. 'Please, let us stay here. One of these men can stay. Please.'

'He comes. They both come,' Malmgren said to Hager. 'She wants her father helped so much, she can tell us who the rest are. Bring her along. She'll talk fast enough. That damned Frenchie'll talk when he sees a noose over his head.'

'My father can't talk. He's unconscious.'

Malmgren shook the Spencer carbine he held in his hand. 'I say he comes, Deputy. We know one of them's wounded. We'll take them. I want all of them together when we do.'

Slattery said, 'Let them stay, Alf. They can't run. Bob will be right here.'

'No! No, you don't pull that!' Malmgren spat. 'Hager, you represent O'Hearn in this. You had that nice soft job of yours 'cause Dan kept you on. Well, I'll tell you. You let them get away with this, I'll see to it O'Hearn don't get one vote next fall and both of you'll be out. You hear that? Now you do your duty.'

Hager stared from Malmgren to LeDuc, then looked helplessly at Marie. 'I'm sorry. You come. You both come.'

'I'll stay,' Bob Clark offered. 'He's bad, Alf. You take the horse and I'll stay.'

Malmgren shifted his stance. Hager said quickly, 'Dan's hit bad. He was. I can't cause him to lose his job.' He shook his head again, surer of what he was doing. 'You hurry up. Both of you.' He backed away from the gathering and walked toward Bob Clark's horse. Malmgren, Rachins and Keelin stepped briskly behind him, with Jesse trailing them. Marie moved to go after the deputy.

Bob Clark touched her arm. 'Won't do any good. Hager's in charge.'

'But my father isn't part of this holdup.' Marie stared at the blackened, smoking ruins. 'He wasn't a part of this. He couldn't be a part of it.' She looked directly into Slattery's face. 'He'll die. My father will die if we try to keep up.'

Slattery said, 'He wouldn't live the night out here, Marie. Not without any cover. He's having a hard enough time breathing. The smoke would kill him.' He nodded to the Clarks. 'How about another house? How far is the first ranch on this side?'

'Two miles,' said Will Clark. 'Rolf Argrew's spread is 'bout two, two and a half miles.'

'We'll leave him there,' Slattery said. He turned to Marie. 'You'll ride slow and easy. Don't worry about Hager and Malmgren. You'll stay at that first ranchhouse. I promise you.'

95

Nodding to the Clarks, Slattery said, 'Take as much time as you need.' He watched Marie LeDuc kneel down beside her father, then walked to where he'd left King. Hager and Rachins had mounted ahead of Malmgren. They'd left Jesse in the roadway and had headed onto the trail. Malmgren sat his saddle rigidly, not saying a word while Yeager and the last three posse members mounted. He watched LeDuc's horse and the Clarks, who lifted the wounded man. Keelin studied the ruins, spitting a mouthful of saliva into the dying embers. The stench of the burned horses was enough to sicken anyone's stomach, yet if even part of one building was still up, Slattery would have made Hager leave the wounded man and his daughter. But with the wind, the freezing cold, and no protection, they had to move. It would have been useless to push Hager any more, the state the deputy was in.

Slattery swung King and rode to where Jesse still stood. 'You want to come along?' he asked the boy. 'I'll ride double.'

Jesse's head moved from side to side. 'I'll bury them,' he said. He stood stiffly, his gangling arms hung at his sides as if some force beyond his control held them there. 'I'll go down when I finish.'

Slattery nodded. 'Jesse, you didn't get a look at any of those men? Or the clothes they were wearing?' He flicked a glance at Marie LeDuc, well beyond earshot. 'The one who was shot?'

'I don't know. They were only cowhands to me. All I know is I woke up and found Mr and Mrs Macrina. I dragged them out 'fore the fire got them. That's all I know.'

Slattery said, 'You take care of them, Jesse. We'll tell the Argrews that you'll be coming down.' He paused before he kneed King. Most of the clouds had blown off to long, streaky scud that shone yellowish white in the light of the huge full moon. Marie was up in the saddle behind her father, the Clarks waited alongside them to keep abreast while they rode. Slattery wasn't certain they'd catch the men they were after. If they did, he wasn't certain he could stop Malmgren and the rest from going hog wild. Especially when they joined with Charlie Shields and the men he had with him. But Slattery was certain of one thing: LeDuc and his daughter would be left at Argrew's. Innocent or guilty, the old man was too far gone to last much longer. Marie didn't deserve one bit of what she'd already had to stand. Hager would have to see that.

* * *

Alf Hager kept his mount right behind the six riders ahead of him. He could hear Slattery's black clopping and snorting like the rest of the animals while they went down the steep grade. Malmgren had been talking to the men all the time they'd been riding, but Hager couldn't

97

make out what was being said. Every so often one of them would glance back at him, then they'd talk again among themselves or shake their heads short, showing they'd completely lost confidence in him. Hager knew Slattery had, too. Yet Slattery stayed right on his tail to protect him; a man like Slattery could tell who'd be good in a fight. Even back there with the LeDucs, Slattery had tried to help. He had. He had tried out in front of the jail when the posse was formed, and at the LeDuc shack, stepping out in the open like that....

Alf Hager shook his head. He was lost and flustered. He wanted to drop behind and talk to Slattery, to ask him to take over. But he didn't dare, not since Jake Malmgren had made that threat about Dan O'Hearn. Jake could swing the election for someone else, and it would be his fault for letting Dan down. Hager shook his head again. It didn't help his headache. The slow, steady thumping across his forehead had started when he'd first smelled the stink of the dead horses. Bad enough the way Robby Malmgren had been killed. Then they left Lou and his wife in the house to burn like the animals. He and the men never would have found out if Jesse hadn't been left for dead, too.... They'd gone a quarter-mile already. Hager stared up at the broken shadows of the forest against the towering black overpowering presence of the mountain, the patches of snow showing above the trees, the huge watching creatures standing straight up and seeming to move with each step of his horse. There were so many hiding places. The murderers could wait up there and watch until they were in the exact right spot. They could. The trail descended sharply toward the foothills, the pine branches overhanging the trail in spots like a trellis, shutting out the moonlight. You could feel only the wind, the icy wind that pounded in your ears and shut out all sound. A gun could bang, six could, and you wouldn't even have as much warning as the Macrinas had.

Behind him Slattery said, 'Anything wrong, Alf?'

'Nothin' wrong. Nothin' wrong.'

'Your horse is slowing. You sure he hasn't picked up a stone in his shoe?'

Hager stared at Slattery in the darkness, under the creaking of the pines. The horseshoes hardly even sounded here, the pine needles were so thick. Like a blanket. He wished he could lie down and pull a blanket over him. Right out here. He felt like laughing, thinking of it like that. He felt safer though, with Slattery riding alongside him now.

'You think it could be a stone?' Slattery was asking again, and Alf Hager answered quickly, 'No. No stone. I was just resting him.'

Slattery studied him. 'We'd better pull up. They've slowed ahead.'

'We'd better,' Hager agreed. He could see

99

that the others had almost stopped. They were bunched together, the words they spoke so low and held down he couldn't catch a phrase. They could be laughing at him, or there was a chance the killers had stopped and were waiting. One of them was wounded. They'd taken the time to go into Macrina's because Rob had hit one of them. They could be hiding to put up a fight. Alf Hager tightened his fingers on the reins, and fell a little behind Slattery.

Slattery noted the deputy had fallen back. The man spoke so oddly, he had to be watched. Slattery angled King to the right, directly in front of Hager's mount, so he could cover the lawman if there was trouble.

*　　*　　*

Malmgren was doing the talking. The men circled around his horse, muttering words of agreement. 'I smell it, too,' Rachins said calmly. 'Only there's no cabin up in there, Jake.'

'There's caves. Could be from a cave. There's enough cover up there.'

'It's comin' from high up,' Keelin said. Gassen, Wetterholm, and Yeager spoke out in agreement. 'It's not just wood smoke. There's something else, too.'

Jake Malmgren swung out of the saddle. One boot was still in the stirrup when he

100

noticed Alf Hager approaching the group. 'Someone's up there.' He held his voice down and gestured at the thick stand of pine which rose black and silent on the left side of the trail. 'I'm having a look-see. You comin', Hager?'

Before Hager could answer, Slattery said quietly, 'I'll go with you. The deputy should be where he can handle everyone.'

'I'll go too.' Gil Rachins handed the reins to Keelin.

'Two of us is enough,' Slattery said. 'More would make too much noise.' He slid his 73 Winchester from its boot, saw that Rachins was climbing out of the saddle anyway. 'Two's enough, Rachins.'

Gil Rachins was on the ground, both booted feet planted firmly. He reached up to take his carbine. 'Jake first, then you and me.'

'You stay here,' Slattery said. He held the Winchester across his lap, the muzzle inches from Rachins' head. 'I've had you behind me once too often. Malmgren and I go. You stay.'

Rachins looked at Malmgren. 'Jake?'

Malmgren stared directly at Rachins. 'You stay, Gil. Anyone is up there, we'll all be goin' after him.' He added to Alf Hager, 'That's right, isn't it, Alf?'

Hager was silent, his attention on the trees. He sniffed audibly, as though he tried very hard to breathe in the air. 'I don't smell anythin',' he said. 'I don't.'

'I do,' Malmgren said. 'We'll all move in
101

once we know.' With that he left his horse and walked into the woods.

Slattery watched Alf Hager for a moment. The deputy sat as though he was alone, not talking to anyone, staring down at the ground. Slattery swung around and followed Jake Malmgren into the pines.

CHAPTER TEN

Slattery knew they had something before he'd gone thirty yards. Jake Malmgren was barely visible in the thick pine branches, and only the soft scuff of his boots on the needles told where he moved. The trees broke off into an opening ahead. Moonlight whitened the sandy clearing and stretch of rock face that ran for eighty or ninety feet before the trees started again. The smoke could almost be felt. Malmgren had taken the correct action when he'd stopped the horses. The trail below, where the posse waited, would be a wide-open shot from the rocks. Even with the wind, anyone on lookout would hear the snorts of the horses, the slap of leather and jangle of jerked bits.

Jake Malmgren whispered, 'See the cave? There, to the left of the rocks.' He'd halted in the cover of a tall pine, crouched down so he could peer beneath the branches. He flattened out, crawled ahead.

Slattery could see the mouth of the cave, a roundish blacker section of stone beyond three huge boulders. Light from flames of a fire flickered inside, low and almost hidden by the boulders.

Malmgren moved to the edge of the trees. He kept crawling. Slattery touched his leg. 'Not too far,' he warned. 'You'll be out in the open.'

Malmgren shook him off. 'Jesse said there's five left. I want to know how many are up there. They all could be.' He started to crawl on.

Slattery held Malmgren's arm. 'We've got enough men to circle them.' His fingers tightened on the leather coatsleeve. The halo of light had brightened momentarily, as though something that burned quickly had been put on the fire. Grayish smoke showed over the boulders, the fire-flicker coming through it like moonlight through a thin edge of cloud. Slattery rolled onto his side and drew a cartridge out of his right coat pocket. Still lying on his side, he arched the bullet high in the air at the cluster of boulders.

Dead quiet for seconds, then the small ping of the cartridge as it struck the stone below the cave mouth. It bounced off and made a soft plop landing in the sand.

Nothing moved at the cave entrance. Malmgren crawled ahead another foot. He froze when a figure appeared at the boulders.

The lone man leaned against the center rock,

using it as cover while he crouched to look outside. The rifle he held was ready, Slattery knew, from the angle he held it. Jake Malmgren's arm dropped down to draw his sixgun. 'I'll get him,' he whispered.

'Don't,' Slattery said. 'He could duck back in.'

'I won't miss.'

'Don't. If they're all in there, it'll take a good long time to get them out. We have to be sure.'

Malmgren muttered a curse. 'He could be the one who killed Robby.' He didn't draw, just watched with Slattery. The man had satisfied himself the noise he heard was no threat. He turned his back to the trees while he stepped inside.

'Dammit, I want him,' Malmgren said softly. 'I'll get him. Every one, I'll get.'

Slattery slipped back under the pine branches, crawling several yards before he stood. He waited until Jake Malmgren was erect beside him, then with one hand out in front he pushed the branches ahead away from his face. He made certain Malmgren didn't fall behind. He'd known well enough what the man was capable of since he'd shot LeDuc. Malmgren had just as strong a drive to kill as the men they hunted. He would've killed that man despite the warning it would have given the others. Jake Malmgren would kill any man when he felt he had to, and Tom Slattery didn't want that kind of man at his back.

104

'Hold it down,' Gil Rachins ordered. 'Shut up till they get back in.' He looked at Alf Hager as though he expected the deputy would add to that, but Hager simply kept staring down at the ground.

Hager heard the small talk around him. 'They could all be in there,' Gassen said. Wetterholm said, 'We shouldn't've split the posse. We need every man Charlie Shields took with him.' Hager heard the words, and that was all. He kept glancing around at the LeDucs and the Clarks waiting with them. He pressed his boots into the stiffened mud, not quite frozen despite the chill and cold. He lifted a foot and pushed it down hard beside the holes he'd already made. He intended to count to ten before water under the surface seeped into the last hole. By the time he got to nine, small heel-holes dotted the ground around him. The moonlight made them seem dark and deep, and he didn't feel like making any more. The rifle he held was a heavy weight in his hand. He didn't want to go up in the rocks, nor did he want to stand here and talk. The waiting got on his nerves. The long descent into the valley stretched out ahead of him. There'd be shooting now, if the gang was up in the rocks. The thought of what could happen knotted his insides. The icy chill went through him, and it was hard for him to even think of what was in the rocks or down in the valley.

Malmgren and Slattery broke from the trees. They walked fast. Because he was in the group, Alf moved with the others to meet them. If he'd faced some of the responsibilities with Dan O'Hearn, maybe it would be different now. It was Dan's fault really, because he'd allowed him to have it so soft, doing janitor work, not ever taking him along when he arrested a drunk. Alf stepped in closer to Malmgren and Slattery so he could hear the talk. It was Dan O'Hearn's fault. He could change that by doing something big in taking the killers. But he was scared. He was so terribly scared.

'. . . we only could see one,' Malmgren was saying. 'The cave's 'bout ten, fifteen feet across the front. The rocks'll give them plenty cover.'

'The rocks will help us, too,' Slattery added. 'They block the entrance, and we can move in from both sides without being seen.' He nodded toward the Clarks and the LeDucs. 'They can stay right here. Eight will be enough. Three circle in around from each side, two from the front.'

'I'll take the deputy with me in front,' Malmgren said. 'Wetterholm, Yeager, and Gassen on the left. Rachins, you and Keelin go with Slattery on the right.'

'Good.' Gil Rachins hefted his carbine, banged the stock against his leg. 'Slattery, you know the way. You go first.'

Slattery eyed him for a second, then looked

at Alf Hager. 'You can stay with Bob Clark. His father'll come with us.'

'Hager comes,' Jake Malmgren argued. 'The law should be with us. We're goin' to get them out of there. I don't care whether it's walkin or on their backs, but I want it to be strictly legal.'

Slattery held his stare on Hager. 'You can stay here,' he repeated. 'Will Clark will agree to go in.'

'No,' Malmgren snapped. 'Alf, you either appoint one of us head of this posse or come yourself. You do it.'

Alf Hager nodded slowly. 'I'll come,' he said. 'I'll go with you, Slattery.'

'He does not,' said Rachins. 'We do it Jake's way.'

Slattery said, 'I'll go in by the front instead of you, Malmgren.' He watched Rachins and Keelin. 'You'll be with these two.'

Rachins said, 'We do it like Jake wants. Hager'll be safe with him.'

'I take the front with the deputy.' Slattery looked directly at Malmgren, but he couldn't see his expression plainly in the hazy light. He watched Malmgren's slow nod. 'I'll draw them out, same as before, Jake. No one opens up till the deputy decides. No one.'

'Jake?' Rachins edged closer to Malmgren.

Malmgren backstepped toward the trees. He stared at the LeDucs. 'Hager wants to go in with Slattery. Okay. Just as long as those two stay right there when we drag the rest out of

107

that cave.' He swung on his heels and bent over to push past the branches.

'Wait until the deputy gets off the first shot,' Slattery said. 'If we can take them without a fight, we'll do it.' He watched Malmgren going into the pines. Malmgren didn't answer. He kept up his quick stride, with Rachins and Keelin a step behind him.

Wetterholm, Yeager, and Gassen had moved to the left. Slattery lightly touched Alf Hager's hand. 'Stay down low,' he told the deputy. 'We'll stay together all the way.'

*   *   *

'Slattery'll have to be in the open,' Rachins said. 'I can hang back and get him, Jake.'

'Not yet,' Malmgren whispered. He pushed the pine branches aside, held them so they wouldn't swish back and make a noise. 'We don't know how many're in there. We need every man.'

'Look, Jake, we want that money,' said Rachins. 'We won't get it with Slattery alive.' Keelin, crouched low next to Rachins, could see the dark mouth of the cave beyond the huge boulders. 'Jake's right, Gil. We can use every man we have goin' in. One of us gets to the money first, the rest back him up.'

'How, Jake? As long as Slattery's—'

'That's enough! Enough!' Jake Malmgren whispered. He'd reached the spot he'd wanted,

108

fifty feet from the boulders. Rachins' griping irritated him. He wanted the men who killed his brother, and all Rachins was here for was the money. The fact that Gil didn't give one thought to the kid or how he'd been shot without a chance grated on Malmgren's mind. Jake wanted only to see the murderers stretched out in front of him. He'd use Hager, Slattery, anyone as long as he got that. They'd take the money, but it wasn't the important thing. Jake dropped flat under the pines at the edge of the clearing. He could barely see the flicker of the fire from the cave. The moon was like a floodlight, white on the stones and sand. He couldn't see any movement in the spot where Slattery and Hager would be or in the shadows beyond the cave. He lay still, absolutely quiet, watching.

'Hager should've done somethin' by now,' Rachins said beside him.

'Shut up! Damn you, shut your damn mouth!' Malmgren snapped. The low ping of a cartridge striking the rocks had sounded. And in the tense silence the bullet Slattery had thrown plopped in the sand. 'They'll show,' he whispered. 'Ready! Get ready!'

CHAPTER ELEVEN

Tom Slattery pressed the stock of his Winchester into his shoulder while he stared into the mouth of the cave. The noise the .44 shell had made was louder than the first time. He expected someone would show immediately. Only one man had come out last time. More of them might look out now. Behind him, Alf Hager lay prone on the pine needle blanket under the branches. He hadn't moved. The deputy hadn't even aimed his carbine.

'Stay behind me,' Slattery said softly. 'Keep back till I get past those rocks.'

Hager did not answer. His wide-open eyes stared up at the rocks. The moonlight gave his skin a bleached, whitish tinge. Slattery pulled his own body ahead, leaning on his elbows, tightening his finger on the trigger.

The head and shoulders of a man appeared behind the rocks. There was no sound except the wind in the trees. Slattery waited a few seconds for the man to show more of himself. When the head continued to stay motionless behind cover, Slattery rolled onto his right side and arched another bullet through the air. Quickly, he straightened on his elbows again, centering his gaze on the blurred shadow of the man's hat.

The lead cartridge struck stone with a loud metallic ring. The figure straightened.

'Hold it right there!' Slattery called. 'You're covered on all sides. Don't move!'

A small flash of flame spat from the man's weapon. The bang of the rifle came immediately after, mixed with the crack of a gun on Slattery's left.

The man went down. Weapons exploded to the left and right of the cave, the quick repeated bangs echoing into the trees, bullets smashing with loud cracks against solid rock and ricocheting across the clearing. Slattery was on his feet, running toward the rocks. He was aware of the high, zipping sound and screaming whine of lead slugs, and the shrill terrified screams of horses inside the cave. The dark figures of Malmgren, Rachins, and Keelin charged in from their position. The man who'd been shot beside the boulder hadn't moved. No other gunfire came from the cave. Slattery crouched over to make a poorer target, triggered off a shot, pumped the lever and put another bullet through the mouth to keep anyone inside down while the posse closed in.

Alf Hager, terrified by the gunfire and scream and whine of the ricochets, hugged low to the ground as he ran. He hadn't gotten off a shot, hadn't tried. He kept only a stride behind Slattery, using Slattery's body as a shield for his body. He'd taken just four quick strides

111

before the carbine barrel snagged between his knees, and he tripped and went sprawling, sliding along the hard rocky ground.

*　　*　　*

Bullets from the converging men's weapons pounded into the cave, but no return gunfire came.

Slattery had reached the upgrade, the ground hard and firm under his boots and not as steep as it had seemed from the trees. The wounded man squirmed to push himself erect and grab the carbine he'd dropped. Slattery kept his muzzle centered on him, flicked his eyes to watch the three who charged in on the right. Malmgren made no attempt to cover himself. He triggered off one shot, another, and another, lost in an almost insane drive to get into the cave. Rachins, a step behind him, held his fire, waiting until he had a definite target. Keelin hung back a full stride. He waited like Rachins, watching Slattery as much as he watched the rocks. Horses shrieked and kicked inside the cave, their terror echoing out into the clearing.

Slattery reached the downed man at the same time as Malmgren. The groping fingers held the carbine's stock, but the man didn't have the strength to raise the iron barrel. Slattery bent low, jerked the weapon away and threw it behind him. Malmgren, Rachins, and

112

Keelin had passed the rocks and vanished into the cave. Slattery paused a fraction of a second, motioned to Wetterholm rushing in on his left. 'Check him for a hand gun,' he called. 'Watch him.'

Wetterholm knelt beside the wounded man, started to open his thick sheepskin coat.

Gunfire blasted inside the cave, two shots so close together they boomed in an ear-ringing explosion off the solid stone walls.

Slattery was inside, his Winchester still pumped and leveled. A lone man lay awkwardly in death against the side wall beyond the small fire. Malmgren, his back to Slattery, leaned over the man, looking at his face. Keelin and Rachins had set down their weapons. Fresh wood had been thrown on the fire, and while they waited for it to burn they grabbed for the horses' bridles or bits to calm the animals.

Jake Malmgren whirled to face Slattery, his carbine leveled, his face twisted into a hateful snarl. 'You know him, Slattery? You know this one?'

The man was about thirty, blond with smooth beardless skin. A wide white bandage covered the top of his left side. The bullets Malmgren had put into him made two tiny holes over his heart.

'You know him, Slattery?'

Slattery shook his head. He kept his Winchester as level as Malmgren's, not sure

113

what the man would do. The horses snorted and thumped the dirt floor with their hoofs while they quieted. Keelin had his almost calm. He patted the long neck, turned the animal. 'I've never seen him,' said Slattery. 'Either of them.'

Malmgren did not answer. He stood like a drunk, weaved back on his heels, his eyes burning into Slattery's face. Keelin had the horse completely calm. He'd turned it so he could reach and open the saddlebags.

Malmgren lowered the muzzle. He glanced across his shoulder at Keelin and Rachins. 'Hurry up. The rest are still goin'. We can't wait.'

Slattery backed past the fireplace, followed by Malmgren. Wetterholm had propped the wounded man against the side of a boulder. He'd opened the man's coat and shirt; his entire chest was drenched with blood. Gassen and Yeager crouched close and watched Wetterholm try to halt the flow. The man's dark-bearded face was tilted to one side, his eyes stared blankly. Slattery and Malmgren leaned over him.

'He's bad,' Wetterholm said. 'How's the other one?'

'Finished,' Malmgren told him flatly. He waved the others into the cave. 'Get a look at him, see if you know him. Know this one?'

None of the men did. Gassen and Yeager moved through the mouth. Wetterholm continued pressing his folded kerchief against the wound. Malmgren touched Wetterholm's shoulder. 'Forget him. See if you know that one.'

'He'll bleed to death.'

'Get inside,' Malmgren snapped. He yanked Wetterholm to his feet and pushed him past the boulders. Malmgren bent over the dying man and grabbed his thick growth of black hair. 'Where'd the rest go,' he questioned. When the man only groaned, he shook the head from side to side. 'Where?'

'Let him alone,' Slattery said.

Malmgren's head whipped around. 'Damn you!'

'Let him go.' Slattery's right arm shot out. His fingers tightened on Malmgren's and ripped the hand free. The man's head drooped onto his left shoulder. He moaned.

The firelight in the cave flared high as the fresh wood caught, and the entire mouth brightened.

Malmgren straightened, his carbine poised like a heavy club. Slattery turned his back on him and knelt to study the man's wound. He heard Malmgren utter an obscene curse and then call, 'Clark! Will Clark! Bring them two in here! Bring them in!'

Slattery had drawn his handkerchief from his side pocket. He couldn't save the man, he knew. A low pained groan came as he pressed the cloth hard against the wound bare inches

115

from the throat.

He heard Rachins say behind him, 'There's nothin' on the horses, Jake. We checked the rolls and saddlebags.'

Keelin added, 'That one inside was in on that holdup. I know his coat and hat. I c'n swear to that.'

'Know him?' asked Malmgren.

'No. But he was there. This one, too. I couldn't see their faces 'cause of the bandannas. But they were there.'

The sound of walking horses approached the clearing. Malmgren called out. 'Hurry up, Clark! Get them in here 'fore they're both dead! Bring our horses in!' He squatted down alongside Slattery. 'He's gotta talk! I'll make him talk!'

'He can't talk now. If I can keep him alive, we can question him later.' He touched the man's jaw, eased the head straight. The eyes were closed. Spittle and blood showed at the side of his mouth.

Slattery could hear quick words in the clearing. Alf Hager's voice was loud as he shouted to someone on the horses.

Rachins stared toward the horses. 'There's no money in there, I tell you, Jake. We looked every place.'

'Forget the money,' Malmgren said. 'Drag LeDuc in here.'

'But they must've stashed it some—'

'To hell with the money! I said get LeDuc

116

before this rotten killer dies! They know where the rest went! I want to know!'

Rachins hurried toward the horses. Alf Hager talked a steady stream and laughed. A quiet voice answered the deputy. Slattery recognized the speaker. He looked around at Augustin Vierra. The Mexican and a cowhand wearing a leather jacket and sombrero also rode with the Clarks and LeDucs. Jake Malmgren grunted when he saw them and, along with Slattery, stared at Alf Hager's face.

Blood, sand and pine needles caked the deputy's forehead and the left side of his face from ear to jawline. The deputy grinned widely, foolishly, and proudly at them. 'We got them,' he said stepping onto the rise ahead of the horses. 'We did! We got them!'

Augustin nodded, unable to fathom the thin man's exuberance. Will Clark led the LeDucs' mount onto the rise in among the boulders. Marie sat tired and fearful in the saddle. She supported the whole weight of her father, whose eyelids didn't as much as flutter.

Augustin Vierra said, 'I came when I was told, Tomas. We were with the herd.'

Slattery nodded. 'Help the girl down, Gus,' he said. Malmgren shook his head. 'Let them stay so this one can see.' He placed one hand roughly under the wounded man's jaw and pushed his head back against the rock. 'You know this one LeDuc?' he said. 'He's one of your gang.'

117

The man moaned, opened his eyes, then shut them.

'You know him!' Malmgren snapped. 'You do! You know him and you know where the rest went! You'll tell us! You will!'

Slattery said, 'Malmgren, leave him alone.'

'Will not! I will not!' He pressed the head harder against the stone. 'Tell us, you! You tell us!'

Slattery gripped Malmgren's hand to pull it away. The man's eyes opened and moved slowly across Malmgren's and Slattery's faces. 'Macrina,' he whispered. 'Had ... Macrina had a gun.'

'Where'd they go?'

'Gun ... Macrina ... shot ...'

Blood suddenly welled up in his mouth and a convulsion shook his body. Malmgren swore at him. 'Where'd they go? Where?' He cursed again, seeing he was dead, and he dropped the head roughly. For a few moments he stared bitterly at the man. Slattery stood, and Malmgren straightened beside him. Alf Hager was saying, 'We got them both! I did my job here! I did! One of you'll have to take over, but I did my job!'

Malmgren paid no attention to the deputy. He walked past him to the horses. 'Well, Bob, go in and see if you know the other one. You too, Quinn.'

The man with Augustin Vierra, deep-chested and wide in the shoulders, swung off his horse. His face was wide and long, with a crooked nose that had been broken years before. His jaw was square and stubborn. He did what he was told when Malmgren said, 'Get goin'. Faster. The rest are ahead. We got to get after them.'

Augustin Vierra had both arms raised to lift Eduard LeDuc from the saddle. 'Easy,' he said to Marie in a quiet voice. 'I have him. Let go easy.'

'What you doin' there?' Malmgren questioned. 'Leave him be, you—'

Augustin spoke without glancing around. 'He is very bad. He will die.'

'You're damned right he will. Here or at the end of a rope! You put him back up there, Mex!'

Slattery said, 'Carry him inside, Gus. Use your blankets and the Clarks'. Take my roll, too.' He held his hand up to Marie to help her dismount.

'What is this?' Malmgren said. He looked at Alf Hager. 'You lettin' them do this? We got those two? We can catch the rest!'

Hager nodded his head. 'You can get them. I'm stayin' here. I got shot.' He wiped his hand along his head and face, and the palm and fingers came away caked with grime and blood. 'See. I got shot. I can't lead.'

'What?' Malmgren glanced about at the faces, dumbfounded. 'You fell on a rock. No bullet did that.'

'I was shot.' Hager stared directly at Slattery who was still holding Marie LeDuc's hand while she started into the cave. Slattery watched the girl. 'Stay with your father,' he told her. 'Keep him close to the fire, under the blankets.'

Malmgren took a step toward the girl, then halted as abruptly as he'd moved. 'She comes,' he said bluntly. 'Both her and her old man. I don't care 'bout this crazy deputy. The LeDucs come with us.'

'The LeDucs stay,' said Slattery. He watched how Rachins and Keelin had edged in behind Malmgren, ready to back him. The cowhand named Quinn came out of the cave. He slowed his quick walk when he caught on that something was happening.

'That man inside,' he said to Malmgren. 'He's Crawford's foreman. He was with those cows Shields bought last month.'

Malmgren's stare remained fixed on Slattery. 'You sure?'

'Positive. I helped with the end of the gather. I know him.' He nodded down at the dead man. 'This one I'm not sure about. He could've been at Crawford's.'

Malmgren shook his head. 'I should've seen it. They knew about the money. Shields wouldn't've been smart enough to shut his stupid mouth about takin' the money in cash.'

Slattery said, 'How many cows did Shields buy from this Crawford?'

120

'Five hundred,' Quinn said. 'He paid ten dollars a head and charged you fifteen, mister. Those two knew exactly how much you'd have with you when you came in. They knew exactly when to wait to hit Shields.'

'My father knew nothing about that,' Marie LeDuc said from the cave mouth. 'He only knew Mr Shields planned to have more cattle and wanted us to move in with him.'

Slattery said, 'You stay inside there, Marie. Take care of your father.'

Marie's lovely dark face didn't lose its worry. 'The ones who left the wounded man off will come back for them. If we stay—'

'You're not stayin',' Malmgren cut in. 'I don't let anyone get away after killin' my brother. Your father comes.' He snapped a glance at Slattery and Hager. 'LeDuc comes with us!'

'LeDuc stays here,' said Slattery. 'Augustin, you'll stay along with the Clarks.'

'Me too,' said Hager. He still grinned, confidently, nodding his head vigorously. 'Dan'll understand, after I got hit. He will.'

'Look, Hager—' Malmgren began.

Hager backed away like a hurt child, acting as though he might cry. 'I got hit! I've done my part! I have!' He cowered alongside Slattery. 'You take over, Slattery. Dan told you to take care of me in the office. He'd want you to take over.'

'He would like hell!' said Malmgren. 'It was

121

my brother who was killed! I take over!'

'No, you don't.' Hager backed even further behind Slattery. Rachins snickered disgustedly, but no one else made a sound. All watched the childlike, pitiful actions of Alf Hager. 'I was in charge!' the deputy whined. 'I've been shot, so I say who's in charge! Slattery!'

Malmgren stared at the deputy. Not a word left his mouth. Quinn, Rachins, and Keelin lined up alongside him and waited. Vierra edged toward Slattery. 'I will ride with you, Tomas,' the Mexican said calmly. His right hand rested on his hip above his .32 Remington's butt.

Malmgren nodded, slow and steady in his movements. 'LeDuc and his daughter stay here,' he said, the nod continuing. 'Will, you and Bob'll see to it they don't leave.'

Clark said, 'They'll be here when you get back. We'll all be here.'

Malmgren kept nodding. 'And Slattery's in charge, Alf. You'll back him in everything that happens.'

'Yes! Yes! He'll handle it! Dan'll see I got shot!' Alf Hager grinned at the men and then at Marie. 'This is right! I've handled it right! I've done my job! My job's all done!'

Malmgren's nod stopped. 'All right, then. That's how it is.' His calm eyes told Rachins, Keelin, and Quinn to stay quiet. He motioned at Wetterholm, Yeager, and Gassen, and to

122

Slattery. 'Quinn says there's a line camp Crawford used in the gather. They're holin' up, they'd use that. You decide.'

'We'll look at it,' Slattery said. 'Quinn, you lead.'

Malmgren had already started to walk toward the horses, trailed by the others who'd ride in the posse.

Slattery said to Vierra, 'Take care of those two, Gus.' His glance rested for a moment on Eduard LeDuc, barely visible under the blankets near the fire. Then he spoke to Marie. 'You should sleep. The men will watch for you.'

'Yes,' said Augustin Vierra. 'We will not leave you.'

Marie studied the figure under the blankets, then looked at Alf Hager who'd gone out to sit beyond the circle of stones which formed the fireplace. 'They were cooking potatoes,' she said to Augustin. 'If you will get a bird in the morning, there will be food.' She glanced toward the trees at the sound of the horses as the men mounted and rode toward the roadway. She looked at Slattery, her eyes tired but soft in the hazy flicker of light. 'Thank you, Tomas.' She walked over to her father.

Slattery watched her and said to Augustin, 'Make her sleep. She might break.' His voice quieted even more. 'Be easy on the deputy.'

'We will.'

The woman had reached her father. She said

123

a few words to Alf Hager, and the deputy moved closer to the fire's warmth. Turning, Tom Slattery walked down the incline toward where King waited in the middle of the moonlit clearing.

CHAPTER TWELVE

The trail leveled off for a hundred yards an eighth of a mile below the cave, then became steeper and rockier as it dropped into the valley below. The wind had died with the clearing sky, leaving the bitter cold that grew harder the lower the posse rode. Slattery had caught up and moved to the head of the column. He'd stayed in the lead all during the descent. He didn't worry about the safety of Marie LeDuc and her father, not with Augustin and the Clarks there to face anyone who showed. LeDuc had looked bad, very bad, and Slattery wasn't certain he'd come through the night. Alf Hager still bothered him. The man was so completely broken it was impossible to tell how he'd come out of it. Slattery had seen men break before. Some became quiet and easy to manage like Alf, others so wild and violent they had to be tied up to keep from hurting themselves or others. He remembered a Kentucky boy, a huge bull of a man who'd cracked at Cemetery Ridge in the war....

Slattery tried to push aside all thought of his past life, though he could remember that July day as plain as he remembered everything that had happened since the holdup. The heat was thick and heavy the day after the rain when Pickett's Virginians marched straight toward Cemetery Wall, dressed right and as tightly packed as the riders behind him. That's what bothered him about how Malmgren, Rachins, Keelin and Quinn stuck so close and kept their talk down. Slattery remembered how Rachins had watched him every step of the way into the cave, and how Malmgren had cut down the man inside. If he hadn't stopped to make sure the wounded man couldn't use his carbine, they would have had a prisoner to question. But he wasn't certain Malmgren or the other three wanted prisoners, Malmgren because he meant to kill every man who'd been in on the killing of his brother. Rachins and the other two, he wasn't sure of. Rachins and Keelin had torn into the saddlebags so wildly, the money was what they were after. The money.... The shooting of Eduard LeDuc, the wild slaughter of the man inside the cave, both sickened him as much as the slaughter that had taken place in that July heat twelve years before.

He pushed thoughts of the war aside. He could do no more about that than he could about what had happened so far, although now, as their leader, he could control the posse's actions. And he would. The pitch was so steep he had to hold King down to a slow walk. He could feel the horse's shoulders and leg muscles strain, his breath coming in the same jerky spurts as when climbing. The four behind him he didn't trust, yet they were no worry while Wetterholm, Gassen, and Yeager rode directly in back of them. If it was the money, they'd have to use all the help they could get to finish the holdup gang first. Then ... Slattery didn't know. He glanced around, saw Wetterholm, Gassen, and Yeager had strung out and were riding out talking. They were family men, each of them with a life that had existed before the holdup. Each was alone with his own thoughts of his wife and kids, and he guarded them selfishly, valuing their privacy, as Slattery had thoughts of his own life. There was something there that offered security and protection, like Judy Fiske back in Calligan Valley, and the ranchers who'd trusted him to drive their cattle—something in a man's life that even out here couldn't be destroyed.

He didn't see that or feel it with Malmgren and the three who stuck so close to him. He'd watch. He wished Charlie Shields hadn't taken so many men with him. It was up to him to watch.

The moon, white and huge and round, made the valley below almost as clear as day. The meadows and broad flat toward the northwest lay like wide light and dark quilt patches, with only the ranch buildings and smaller homesteaders' cabins, some herds of cattle bedded down for the night here and there, and the wide creek cutting through on its way south, breaking the smooth pattern. Slattery could not see the road Malmgren told him about when the rancher pulled in his roan horse abreast of the black gelding. Quinn, who'd also come up alongside when the road widened, agreed with everything Malmgren said.

'The line camp's about four miles south,' Malmgren explained. 'There's three or four buildin's. The cabin's pine log and the shed is rock.'

'That's where we bunked while we made the gather,' Quinn added. 'I know both buildin's inside.'

'Good,' Slattery said. 'You'll show us the layout if they're there.'

'They'll be there.' Malmgren's tone was emphatic. 'If they're not, we know where Crawford's place is.'

Both riders dropped back and Slattery slowed King even more. They'd been out more than twelve hours and could use the rest. He hadn't planned on a stone building. He could lose some of the family men if the killers holed up in there. He'd have to be careful. Very, very careful, and not take one unnecessary chance.

'Careful, I said,' Jake Malmgren was telling the three who rode in line with his roan. 'We've got to finish that gang off and still be careful how we get that money.'

'Easy enough,' Rachins said. 'Slattery'll move in soon as he thinks he has them. We wait till those other three hayshakers are in the open and finish them, too.'

Malmgren swore at him. 'That's all we need, to have just the four of us get out alive. O'Hearn's goin' to have enough questions now, without that.'

'Hell with O'Hearn. We can keep ridin' west this mornin'. I don't have to go back to Beaver Hole.'

'Well, I do,' Malmgren snapped. 'I planned this to build our ranch. Me and Robby.'

Quinn added, 'Shields'd have dodgers out on me if I didn't show. Anyway, you said Shields left with his section 'fore you hit the pass. If he picked up a trail, he could have those twelve men waitin' at the line camp.'

'I still say we'd be smart to hightail it out,' Rachins argued. He glanced at Keelin, his long, square face hidden now that the moon, so bright just a half hour ago, had slipped its lower edge behind the southern rim. 'Damn it, it'll be another hour 'fore we get there. It'll be so dark, Slattery won't even know what hit him.'

Keelin said, 'Gil's right 'bout Slattery, Jake. He didn't cotton to finishin' off the man in the cave. He watched us too close when we was goin' through them saddlebags. We can hold the other three off while we get the money. But not Slattery.'

Jake Malmgren was silent, thoughtful, his eyes on the hazy forms of the horse and rider ahead of him. Slattery didn't trust them, that was damned clear. Yet the man was needed. They outnumbered and outgunned the three still alive of the gang who killed young Robby. But they wouldn't take them if they reached their horses and made the south pass. Their own mounts were washed out from the long ride and hadn't had the rest and water the killers' horses would have. Slattery knew that. He'd push the fight so it'd be quick and decisive. He'd get in fast so he could take some of them alive.

'I could finish him,' Quinn said. 'He figures I'm just Shields' ramrod. All I do is stay at his back.'

'He's right, Jake,' said Keelin. 'He'll watch Gil and me 'cause of the cave. You too.'

'You'll stick with Slattery,' said Malmgren to Quinn. 'You wait till we have every one of those killers. You hear?'

Jake Malmgren watched Quinn nod, then he rode on in silence. Now, as the moon dropped lower behind the peaks, the grayish haze along the valley bottomlands changed to deeper and deeper black. One ranchhouse off toward the north showed a light. The others stayed as dark and still as they'd been. Slattery had reached the bend where the mountain trail turned

129

into a soft meadow lane. The horses behind the black gelding would catch up once they left the solid hardpack and didn't have to be careful not to step into the deep ruts made by the spring runoff. They had an hour, maybe more, to go. That would give the animals time to catch a second wind. There'd be plenty of dark when they reached the Crawford line camp.

CHAPTER THIRTEEN

The moon was down before the next half hour passed. The soft gray of the valley changed to a blackness that hugged the meadows and flat. Higher up along the circle of mountains the countless stars threw a shadowy light that defined the dark lines of the pine forests and silverish snow patches, but didn't light the valley floor. Quinn, who knew the trail to the line camp, drew up with Slattery and showed the way. The creek, which wound like a huge serpent down from the divide, was thickly timbered where it turned south. Willows, alders and aspens, with a spotting of big long-branched cottonwoods, formed a screen that hid the eight horses even while they were still out on the springy grass of the meadows. Slattery rode in silence, allowing Quinn to lead. After an hour they pushed into the brush along the high left bank. They were so close to the southern rim that Slattery could no longer see the shape of the mountain above them, yet he could feel it rolling on and up and blocking out the little starlight they had left.

Quinn slowed his mount, then stopped at the edge of the river bank. 'It's across there,' he said in a low voice. 'A hundred yards, maybe a little further, beyond the brush.'

The riders behind them circled in. Lew Gassen pounded his gloved hands together as he halted the horse. 'Cut that,' Slattery told him. 'They'll have a man on lookout if they're in there.'

Malmgren said, 'We can move 'round on every side. They won't—'

'I want to have a look before we move in,' Slattery said. 'We'll cross, and you'll wait in the trees while Quinn and I see what's there.'

'I'll go with you, too,' said Malmgren. 'I want a look-see.'

'All right. The rest of you will water the horses and give them a rub. Their horses have had a few hours' rest. These mounts aren't a match if they have a chance to run for it.' He led the posse down off the edge and into the stream, letting King pick his way across to the opposite side. Where a sandbar stretched in along under the overhanging cliff-like bank, he stopped and dismounted. He slipped the Winchester from its boot and pumped the weapon while he waited for Malmgren and

Quinn to climb down with him.

'Don't leave here,' he told the posse. 'I want every one of you right here when we get back.'

'What if they spot you?' asked Rachins. 'You three can't cover every buildin'.'

'Stay here till one of us gets back,' Slattery repeated. 'He'll know where we are. I don't want anyone shot by one of you because you don't know where we are.'

He climbed the bank ahead of Malmgren and Quinn. They followed the bend of the stream to the southwest, keeping to the brush and sand, careful not to make noise. After a hundred yards Quinn touched Slattery's arm.

'There,' he said. 'You can make out the chimney. Across the meadow in them trees.'

Slattery strained his eyes. Four buildings, none showing a light, were set in where the ground rose into a low foothill. The cluster of timber behind the barn showed a waterhole or offshoot from the river. He crouched lower and moved carefully ahead until he could distinguish the darker shapes of the buildings from the black of the meadow and trees. The cabin was made of logs with a board shed on one side, corral on the opposite side near the barn and outhouse, both of wood. The stone storehouse was at the rear nearest the timber. It was big enough to hide three men and three horses.

'How about a back door?' Slattery asked.

Quinn said, 'None. There's a window in

132

back, though.'

Slattery nodded. He studied the meadows on three sides, the trees and hill. The difficulty was to form a plan considering the dark, confusing distances. He heard a horse whinney.

'Horses are in the barn,' he said.

Malmgren muttered, 'Bastards. They must feel real safe,' with a deep hate to his words. 'They kill a kid like that and they feel safe. They'll see, damn them! They'll see! Quinn, get the rest.'

Slattery stopped Quinn. 'It looks too pat. I don't like it.'

'Dammit, they feel so safe they're bunked in,' Malmgren snapped. 'We can have them 'fore they know what hit them.'

'No, I don't like it,' Slattery answered. 'If the men who have the money are in there, others could be, too. I don't want—' He silenced when he saw the tiny red glow of a cigarette at the corner of the cabin. Malmgren shifted his feet and Slattery reached out to make sure he didn't fire his rifle. Malmgren's whispering showed he hadn't intended that. 'They've got one lookout, they'll have the horses ready,' he said. 'We'll have to circle them slow.'

Slattery could see the man's form now. He'd been on the opposite side of the cabin, was making a round of the buildings.

'Quinn,' he ordered. 'Stay here. They'll light a lamp if they intend to do anything. If they do, get back to the river.'

133

He moved deeper into the trees and Malmgren trailed him. 'What're you waitin' for?' Malmgren questioned. 'Look, we've got the men. We close in slow and careful, we'd take them.'

'Quiet,' Slattery snapped. 'You let them hear you, they'll run. In this dark, they'd only have to head in all directions and we'd miss most of them.'

The remainder of the posse were bunched on the sandbar. Slattery paused and picked up a stick from the ground before he went down the bank. When he reached the horses he told the men to circle around. Gil Rachins took his mount's bridle and swung the animal so he could mount while he listened.

'Don't climb up,' Slattery said. 'We'll stay right here till we can see what's in there. It's close to four now. In another hour it'll start to lighten.'

'They could clear out by then,' Malmgren argued. 'I'm not takin' a chance on losin' them. Not one of them. I tell you that, Slattery.'

Slattery looked straight at Malmgren's tall, slender figure. 'That's exactly what you could do if you hit them now. Either they'd get away or they'd be able to reach that stone shed. I don't want to lose one man doing this.' He hunkered down and dug dark lines into the grayish sand. 'The cabin is here,' he said, marking an X and scratching in a long, curved line to represent the stream. 'They have a

134

lookout moving around the buildings, the barn, outhouse and the stone shed.' He straightened and pointed at the drawing. 'We'll move in slow and circle the whole area. We give the horses a good rest first. We'll be in position to cover the barn, but I want the horses in shape in case one of them makes a break.'

'They won't get far,' Malmgren said emphatically. 'I want to be in close to make sure of that. I want Rachins and Keelin with me to make sure.'

Slattery shook his head. 'We'll go in pairs. You and Rachins can take the back. Keelin and Wetterholm, the left. Gassen and Yeager the right. I'll be with Quinn in front.'

The other men were perfectly silent as Malmgren said, 'Okay, that's okay with me. You can tell Quinn.'

'I'll tell him,' Slattery said. 'Now, get as rested as possible. They'll have the extra edge of sleep, too. That's all the edge I want them to have.'

CHAPTER FOURTEEN

Pat Quinn rubbed his arms and flexed his hands. It was so cold you'd think it was January or February instead of May. He'd brought only the leather jacket he kept in his roll, not a thick sheepskin or bearskin like the

135

rest of the posse. He hadn't figured on anything like this. When he'd gone to Jake Malmgren with his idea about hitting Shields' money, the whole plan had been laid out so foolproof. He'd believed the holdup would go off smooth and easy, with no one hurt except Shields. And he didn't matter. He didn't pay an honest wage to his cattlehands. He took advantage of everyone he could. His trying to get that young halfbreed daughter of LeDuc's had been something Quinn had expected of him, and the way he'd charged Slattery and the Montana ranchers almost twice the price he paid for the beeves he'd bought from Crawford's Creek. Shields had laughed at that, had said it was business and that was all there was to it. Well, the holdup which had been planned was exactly what Shields deserved. The only trouble was that the men inside the line camp had beat Malmgren to it.

Quinn rubbed his chest and patted his arms again. He stamped his feet, then stopped. He couldn't take a chance on the lookout near the shack hearing him. If he'd only made plans for something like this. He'd been with the Mexican who had come in with Slattery. When they'd gotten the word about the holdup and killing, they'd headed right out after the posse. Quinn was glad Vierra had been left at the cave. He liked the Mexican. Slattery ... He regretted he'd have to be the one who put a bullet into the man, but this was his chance to get away from Shields and start on his own. His share of the twelve thousand would buy a small spread....

Quinn's thoughts died when he thought he heard a sound far off toward the south pass. He stood behind the thickness of a cottonwood trunk, stayed absolutely still and listened. Nothing. He was so tensed up he was getting jumpy. He studied the line camp for a full minute, not taking his eyes from the spot he'd last seen the lookout. If they were changing lookouts, he couldn't tell. He'd been up here close to three-quarters of an hour and he was danged cold. He didn't see any smoke from the cabin chimney, so they'd be cold too. Only they had blankets. He glanced around, across his shoulder. Nothing moved back there. Eastward the tops of the peaks had started to get clearer. Darkness hid the outlines, yet he could tell daylight was coming.

The sound was there again southward, and Quinn's head snapped around. He listened, leaning to the left to catch it. He couldn't be sure. Slowly, easily, he worked the lever of his Spencer carbine. With the sun coming up, they'd be moving in the shack. They could head for the south pass, or go back for the wounded man they'd left in the cave. The two that had been killed hadn't had money on them. They'd have to join up with the others to split the take. Quinn rubbed the carbine's barrel along his stiffened leg. So cold. He kept

137

the cartridge in the chamber in case the killers tried riding out. Or for Slattery. He'd never shot a man in the back. He didn't want to, but there'd be no share for him if Slattery wasn't out of the way.

Quinn tensed up again. The sound was real. Hoof-beats, a horse riding hard from the pass.

Quinn backed from the tree deeper into the brush. He was halfway to the river when Slattery led his horse up onto the bank.

'A rider's headin' for the shack,' Quinn told Slattery. Jake Malmgren, walking his gelding directly behind Slattery's black, said, 'We heard it. You should've stayed watchin'.'

Slattery turned to the men behind them. 'Pair off,' he said. 'Leave the horses here and move into position.'

Gassen and Yeager vanished into the darkness. Keelin and Rachins hung back and watched Jake Malmgren. 'Move, I said,' Slattery ordered. 'If that rider's part of the holdup gang, they'll do their own moving. Quinn, you and I will go in by the front.' He ground-tied King and headed for the edge of the meadow. Jake Malmgren and Rachins followed along with Quinn behind him.

Slattery kept his body low. The first traces of day had lightened the sky beyond the eastern peaks. The sky over Beaver Pass had lost its full blackness, had become bluish-gray with a tinge of red showing against the distant patches of snow. The hoofbeats had held at a steady gallop, the horse and rider still out of sight beyond the cluster of timber to the left of the buildings.

'See anything?' Jake Malmgren said. 'I can't make out a thing.'

'Get into position,' Slattery told him and Rachins. 'You'll be the ones who block the pass. They could be saddling up now and ready to ride.'

'We can't get where we want,' said Rachins. 'That rider's comin' in right past where we'd be. We gotta wait.'

'Yeah,' added Malmgren, 'we'd be in position to stop him if you didn't hold us on that sandbar. We didn't need a rest. What we should've done was hit then. Dammit, you see that?'

A lamp had gone on in the cabin. The shape of the small building was clear to them now that the sun had come up behind the peaks. A man carrying a carbine came around the corner of the barn and hurried to the front of the cabin. He was of medium height and appeared to be heavy-set under his full-length buffalo coat. His face was indistinguishable because of the distance and the up-raised collar which almost met the hat worn low over his eyes. The door was opened before he reached it by a man wearing only trousers and a heavy winter undershirt. The lookout spoke quickly to him and the others inside.

'Damn! Sonofabitch!' Jake Malmgren

muttered. 'They'll get away, Slattery.'

'They won't get away. You move into position. The rider passes you, block off that escape.' Slattery turned away from Malmgren and peered past the cottonwood trunk at the cabin door. He did not see Malmgren reach out and slap one hand quickly against the barrel of Quinn's Spencer. He heard only Malmgren's and Rachin's steps as they went off toward the brush.

Slattery watched the trees, the cabin door. Quinn stepped in beside him as the hoofbeats thumped behind the barn. 'Recognize either of those two?' he asked Quinn.

'The one inside, I think, works for Crawford. I couldn't tell about the other.' He pressed in closer to the tree trunk and watched the cabin with Slattery.

The horse and rider rounded the far corner at a considerable angle, the animal running hard and heavily. Before he reached the cabin, the rider broke into loud, high-pitched shouts, calling the name, 'Trox! Trox!' The remainder of what he yelled was lost to Slattery and Quinn as he turned down into the front yard and began to swing out of the saddle even before he had stopped the animal.

A second lamp had flared inside the cabin, throwing a clean yellow light through the side and front windows. Slattery edged forward, his body low, his attention on the opening door and the rider stepping inside the cabin. He realized that Quinn hadn't left the tree trunk. He looked around, crouched lower to use the long high meadow grass for cover. Pale blue sky, deep reddish along the peaks, shone above and through the tops of the leafless branches. Quinn's face was shadowed, but his expression was clear enough to Slattery. He was either scared or trying to make up his mind, and Slattery moved back toward him.

'Don't wait,' Slattery said. 'Stay with me. They'll be out.'

Quinn shifted the Spencer in his hands. The barrel came up, the black muzzle going no higher than Slattery's chest. 'I'll come,' he answered, his voice low, barely audible. 'Go ahead. I'll come.'

Dead silence fell; Quinn waiting, Slattery fully realizing Quinn wasn't one bit scared. From the shack he heard the sound of a door opening, then the quick raised voices of men.

A gun banged behind the shack from the spot Jake Malmgren would be. A second shot followed. Slattery watched Quinn's eyes, knowing what he intended to do. The cabin door slammed shut. More shots rang out.

Slattery shifted his body as though he meant to turn and move toward the shack. 'Careful,' he said to Quinn. 'There's four of them.' His right side to Quinn, he dropped flat and then rolled fast and hard into the wet cold meadow.

Quinn's first shot blasted, pounding so close Slattery felt the terrific whang in his ear. The bullet sliced through his coat, whapped into the mud. Rolling madly, wildly, praying the long drenching grass and darkness would spoil Quinn's next shot, Slattery gripped the stock and lever of his Winchester, bringing it up to fire.

CHAPTER FIFTEEN

Quinn's second slug burned past Slattery's ear, slapped like a handclap into the spongy wet earth. Slattery stopped rolling, turned on his left side and squeezed the trigger.

Quinn, coming toward him, jerked up straight with the impact, high on the left side of his chest, as though he'd struck a stone wall. He staggered backward, his third shot exploding and zinging high above Slattery's head. On one knee, crouched low, Slattery had the Winchester pumped, ready to finish Quinn. Quinn's body crumbled. He tried to hold his carbine, to work the lever, but he hadn't the strength. The weapon struck the ground a fraction of a second before he hit face first.

Slattery was on top of him. He rolled Quinn over, tore at his jacket front until he had the buttons ripped off and Quinn's sixgun in his hand. He hurled the revolver toward the shack. Quinn made no attempt to reach for the carbine, and Slattery shoved him down hard.

In the semi-darkness Slattery felt for the wound and touched the warmth of slippery blood below the collar bone. He grabbed Quinn's right hand, jerked it up and pressed between the wound and heart. The quick, heavy gunfire hadn't slackened. Malmgren and Keelin shouted to each other from opposite sides of the shack.

Slattery said, 'Why'd you try that, Quinn?'

The cattlehand grimaced, pressing the hand stiffly below his shoulder. He glanced toward the shooting, his head cocked to hear the yelling.

'Why, Quinn?'

'You got a rep, Slattery. You—'

'That's not it! Why?' He'd shifted around, closer to Quinn's head, to watch the small log cabin. Barrel flashes spat from the windows he could see. No shadows were clear behind the glass since they'd killed the lamplight. 'Why, Quinn?'

'Go to hell!' Quinn spat. He made an attempt to roll away from Slattery. But he was too weak, and could only lie back and gasp for breath.

Slattery crawled past the prostrate man. Quinn had no gun. He couldn't go far, so he was no worry. Slattery kept his head low, watched the windows and doorway. He had to stop the firing. He wasn't positive the men inside were the ones they were after.... He sprawled out flat, cupped one hand at his

143

mouth. 'You men in the cabin!' he called. 'In the cabin! We're a posse from Beaver Hole! If you're not the ones who held up Shields, stop shooting! We'll hold our fire! Stop shooting!'

A rifle banged from the near window, another from the side. 'Stop!' Slattery repeated. 'Malmgren, Rachins, Keelin, hold your fire!'

The shooting died to his right. Malmgren and Rachins didn't cease fire. Slattery yelled. 'Hold it! Malmgren! Rachins! Hold it!'

Malmgren answered him, cursing loudly, but he and Rachins didn't fire another bullet. A gun banged from the rear window of the cabin, a second at the side.

'In the cabin!' Slattery called again. 'We're holding our fire! We want only the men who held up Shields!' Tense, drawn-out silence rose all around the cabin. The single sound was a drumming of horses hoofs in the direction of the pass. The hazy dawn light had filtered down into the valley, giving the timber along the stream definite shape. Slattery could see the lead horseman, knew from how he sat the saddle and his long cowhide coat that the man at the head was Shields. He cupped his hands to his lips. 'Throw out your guns!' he ordered. 'Step out one at a time! Hands above your heads!'

The cabin door suddenly cracked open. The muzzle of the long black barrel which jutted out flashed in a small flame of fire. The bullet

144

buzzed inches over Slattery's head as the man who'd opened up on him made his dash for the barn. Bent low, crouched almost to the ground, he hugged the cabin side. Covering fire came from the cabin. Guns answered on Slattery's left.

'Low! Aim low!' Slattery called, hearing the rifles pound, aiming his carbine at the legs. The runner faltered in full stride and began to stumble. He tried to stay on his feet and keep running. Then a weapon banged, and the man fell to the earth and lay still.

The door had slammed shut. A shadow moved across the bullet-shattered side window. Slattery fired, and saw the head jerk away out of sight.

The riders were all clear of the pass. The three directly behind Charlie Shields turned right toward Malmgren and Rachins. The midsection swung wide to pass behind the cluster of timber and buildings and help close off the west side of the cabin. Three horsemen at the tail end had already begun to stop their mounts between the buildings and the pass. Slattery gave a quick glance behind him. Quinn hadn't moved from the spot where he'd left him.

'You're surrounded!' Slattery yelled. 'Throw out your guns! Throw them out!'

The outbreak of gunfire from the men of Shields' posse drowned his words. The weapons banged, pounded, a heavier Sharps

50 someone had brought along boomed like a cannon. Slattery crawled ahead through the meadow, careful not to shake the grass and give away his position. The shots from the cabin hadn't slackened. Weapons fired on either side of him now. Grass shook and bent where men crawled to help him close off the front.

Meric Wetterholm slipped in alongside him. He triggered off a bullet and pumped his carbine's lever. 'Shields had two men quit on him. Voss and Wells. But the rest are here. We've got them,' he said excitedly. 'They haven't got a chance.'

'I want them alive,' Slattery said, seeing a lamp suddenly flare on in the cabin.

At that moment the bang of a rifle exploded from the grass. The cabin darkened for an instant after the lead slug smashed the glass and splattered the ignited coal oil. The shooting ceased abruptly within the log building. Fire had caught along the walls, on the floor. The men's figures were visible in the leaping flames. They moved about the interior, dodging as best they could from the windows and still be able to fight the fire.

Gun blasts from the encircling men lessened, breaking off gradually until only one or two still tried to hit their prey.

Slattery pushed himself erect. He straightened, and the men in close to him stood with him.

146

'Stop shooting!' Slattery called. 'Malmgren, Rachins! That's enough!'

'They ain't gettin' out of this,' Malmgren answered. 'We got them now! We ain't lettin' them get away!'

'They won't get away.' The sky was pale blue, the soft light of morning penetrating the trees. Cautiously, slowly, the posse members had showed themselves. Smoke poured from the cabin windows. Bright reddish-orange flames licked up from around the stone chimney, giving a growing, jumping light to the yard and meadow and buildings. The front door opened inward.

'Don't shoot!' a voice yelled. 'We'll come out!'

'You'll come out dead!' Malmgren shouted back. He had his rifle up, ready.

'You shoot,' Slattery warned him, 'you'll go back tied up! You men! Charlie Shields! He doesn't shoot!'

'Please! Please!' the voice screamed through the doorway. Flames penetrated the roof with a cracking, crackling noise and leaped into the air. 'Don't shoot! We give up! Don't shoot!'

'Throw your weapons out!' Slattery ordered. 'File out one at a time! Hands high!'

He walked toward the building, feeling the intense heat against his face. Two rifles, then a third carbine, sailed through the doorway. Three revolvers followed. The heavy-set man came out first, followed by a second and a third

147

who walked more carefully than the other two. The right sleeve of his heavy cowhide coat hung empty down his side. All three coughed and gasped for fresh air. Malmgren, Rachins and Keelin closed in on them.

'Back,' Slattery warned. 'Don't touch them.'

'The money?' Rachins said. 'Where's the money?'

'Money? What money?' the lead man answered. He went into a fit of choking coughs.

The man behind him said, 'Trox is right. We ain't got no money. We don't know nothin' 'bout no money.'

'You had it, damn you. You had it.' Rachins ran toward the burning cabin with Keelin directly behind him. The rear half of the interior was a mass of flames, but Rachins went inside. Keelin hung back, hesitating at the doorway.

Jake Malmgren stopped in front of the man called Trox. 'You held up Shields! You killed my brother! All of you!'

Trox's choking had settled to a grating rasp in his voice. He shook his head. 'No! No, we didn't hold no one up! We were in the cabin when someone started shootin'! We—'

'We chased one of you all night,' Charlie Shields said. He pointed with his uninjured arm to the horse that fed on the grass at the edge of the meadow. 'He led us right here. Damn you, don't try talkin' your way out of this.'

'He won't!' yelled Jake Malmgren. 'None of them will!' He brandished the carbine, jabbed Trox's chest with the muzzle threateningly. 'Shields followed that horse! The rest of us tracked you here! You'll damnwell hang for killin' the kid!'

'And for the Macrinas,' Lew Gassen added. 'You killed them, too. Jesse will identify you. He'll say in court it was you.'

The shorter cowhand behind Trox looked worried. He edged away from the weapon Malmgren held, bumped into his companion with the heavy cowhide coat and empty sleeve. 'No,' he offered weakly, 'Jesse couldn't say anythin'. He didn't see us.'

A loud crash made everyone—the circle of quiet, angry-faced men with guns aimed and the three who'd escaped the holocaust—turn to the cabin. Gil Rachins had backed outside. His hat smoldered. A small line of flame licked along his shoulder where the caving-in roof had brushed him. Keelin slapped wildly at the flame to put it out.

Rachins held a piece of scorched brown canvas. The letters CODY NAT were clear to everyone. Rachins waved the canvas high, looking hatefully at the trio. 'They burned it!' he said, his voice snapping like a whip. 'It's all in there! Every last dollar thrown around, burnin'. On the floor! On the table! It's burnin' up! This is all I could reach!'

'No—' Trox began. He shut his mouth as

Jake Malmgren swung out with the butt of his carbine, catching him full in the pit of his stomach. 'You rotten bastard killers! You'll pay for it! You'll pay! Damn you, we oughta string you up now!'

'String them up!' Gil Rachins echoed savagely. 'I say we string them up!' He moved in alongside Malmgren, with Keelin a step behind him. 'Get ropes! You men, get ropes!' Men left the rear of the circle and went to their horses.

The angry, cursing posse members closed in on the trio, reaching out and grabbing them. Four held Trox. The men who had the other two started to drag them past the cabin toward the cluster of trees.

Slattery moved fast, out in front of the mob. 'No,' he ordered. 'We take them back to Beaver Hole. They'll hang, but they get a trial.'

'Hell with a trial!' Jake Malmgren bellowed. 'They did the killin', all right! We know that! They hang now!' He lifted the carbine, threatening to slam it into Slattery's face.

Slattery didn't budge. 'No lynching,' he said. His Winchester was aimed directly at Malmgren's heart. 'Back—don't try it.'

Malmgren paused. The men who'd gone for the horses rode at a gallop into the yard. Hoofs kicked and squelched in the mud while they pulled their animals to a halt. One threw a coiled rope toward Meric Wetterholm. The cattlehand caught it and waved it above his head.

'We got them! We decide! Damn them, they deserve hangin'!'

The men who held Trox dragged him forward. Then the other two were shoved toward where Slattery blocked the way. The wounded one was bent over unsteadily, his bearded head hung low. He stumbled in the direction of the trees, offered no fight while hands grabbed at him, tearing his hat from his head, ripping the heavy empty-sleeved cowhide coat off his slouched shoulders.

The instant the coat came off, the posse froze. Some swore. Others simply gasped or coughed when they saw the man's checkered red and black shirt. Malmgren, in the middle of the mob, stiffened. He raised his Spencer carbine, held it out in front of him.

Slattery said to the wounded man, 'When did you get shot?'

Trox said, 'He got hit inside the cabin. He tried to put out the lamp and a slug got him. That lamp wouldn't've been lit—'

'Let him talk for himself.' Slattery moved in next to the wounded man. 'When?'

'You tell him, Fenn,' Trox said. 'They got no right takin' us like this. Mr Crawford'll—'

Slattery swung around, his Winchester's barrel high, ready to slam Trox's head. Trox ducked back, quieted. Slattery lifted the empty checkered sleeve. 'You want it rough, mister. Just lie to us.' Nodding to the watchers, he

151

tightened his voice. 'Where'd you get hit?'

Fenn's deep-lined face slackened. 'In Beaver Hole,' he answered. 'I was spotted at the bend.' He edged closer to Slattery at the mutter and movement which followed. Malmgren said, 'What? No, that was LeDuc!' The wounded man nodded his head vigorously. 'I was there. I was spotted there in case something went wrong. I didn't kill anyone though. I didn't.'

Trox swore at him and tried to break away from the men who held his arms. 'You rotten liar! He wasn't there! None of us were!'

He was jerked back and held. The posse members didn't look at him now, but at Malmgren. Jake Malmgren shook his head, staring right into Fenn's eyes. 'We shot the one Slattery hit at the bend. He was in a cave. We killed him.'

Fenn watched the listeners, not sure at all what they'd do. The heat of the flames scorched his backside, and the smoke made him gasp. He didn't dare move away from Slattery. 'Baynes was shot at the Macrinas. Lou Macrina tried drawin' a gun when Trox caught his nigra in the barn. Macrina winged Baynes before Baynes shot him.'

Malmgren's stare didn't leave Fenn. He studied the checkered shirt, his stubbled jaw tight, his eyes set. 'No—no,' he said. He looked around him. There was nothing friendly in what he saw, nor was it encouraging. Rachins and Keelin were both headed for the horses.

152

The solid ring of faces had changed, a new kind of dissatisfaction, hate and bewilderment showing. Malmgren shifted his feet and hit his rump against the man behind him. The man wouldn't budge.

Slattery said. 'I'll take that carbine, Jake.'

Malmgren's head moved from side to side. 'I don't give it up. Not to you.' He jerked the barrel wildly at the men on either side of him, at the ones behind him. They hurriedly opened a path. He watched Slattery, shifted the carbine's muzzle to him. 'No. Robby was killed. He didn't have a chance. I thought LeDuc—'

'You men in back,' Slattery ordered, 'hold Rachins and Keelin.' He made a move to follow Malmgren, who'd sidestepped clear of the posse. Twenty yards behind him Quinn had crawled through the high lush grass toward the horses. Quinn reached the closest, a big white-stocking stallion. His hands were on the stirrup. He strained to pull himself erect and up into the saddle. Malmgren was ten feet from him, headed for the same horse.

Slattery quickened his stride behind Malmgren. Two of the posse moved to circle out toward Malmgren. 'Stay back,' Slattery warned them. Then Malmgren swung around and fired once in the direction of the moving men, and all the posse members ducked down, scattering, the ones holding the three prisoners throwing them to the ground. Slattery kept walking, his eyes on the weapon Malmgren pointed at him.

'Don't try it, Malmgren,' he called. 'You've got to turn to ride. I'll cut you out of the saddle.'

Not answering, Malmgren raised one hand to grip the horn. He bumped into Quinn, on his feet now, trying to lift one boot into the stirrup. Malmgren said something quick and hard to him. Quinn answered as fast, each man's words inaudible to Slattery.

'Get away!' Malmgren suddenly screamed. He let go of the saddle horn, dropped his open palm to Quinn's chest and shoved him away. Quinn stumbled against the stallion's flank as he tried to stay on his feet. Malmgren turned the animal to swing aboard.

'That's enough, Malmgren,' Slattery warned. Alone now, clear of the posse members, he aimed the Winchester. 'You face LeDuc in Beaver Hole.' The finger on the trigger tightened.

He didn't have to shoot. Malmgren, his back to Quinn, couldn't see the cattlehand hadn't fallen. Quinn steadied on his feet and lunged forward, arms and hands outstretched. He landed on Malmgren's shoulders and brought him to the ground. Frightened by the sudden act the stallion wheeled its stern and reared up. Malmgren, the carbine gone from his hands, half wrestling, half fighting to break free of Quinn's arms, rolled away wildly to keep from

154

being stomped.

Slattery moved in and stood above the pair. Cursing hatefully, Malmgren threw Quinn off. He pushed up onto one knee, glared from Quinn to Slattery. 'They won't hang me!' he snarled. 'Robby was killed! By them!' His eyes flashed to Quinn again. 'You, damn you! Damn, damn you!'

Quinn lay on his side, blood drenching his shirt-front. 'You tried to kill me,' he said. 'There was three horses. You get out of the killin', there'll be the holdup you planned.' He exhaled a long wheezing breath. 'I'll tell, damn you.' He looked at Slattery and the men who circled him. 'Rob was ridin' shotgun to help Rachins, Keelin, Voss and Wells hit the buggy. But that gang hit first.'

Malmgren swore at him. 'Bastard. Stinkin' liar. No one's goin' to believe—'

'They'll believe me. I'll talk enough so's they'll believe me.' Quinn took a deep breath. He groaned when the men bent over him and gripped his arms to pull him to his feet. Three others were holding Malmgren. Slattery turned to the burning cabin.

Charlie Shields and eight of the posse had Rachins and Keelin. Keelin walked ahead of Shields, his arms stretched high above his head. Rachins was being held by two men, one on his right side, the second gripping his left arm. Thick, tar-smelling smoke billowed from the flaming ruins. It filled the yard and, swept

155

by the wind, blocked out the golden yellow-orange sunlight that made the wet green of the grass far out in the meadow shine and sparkle.

Shields jabbed his rifle into Keelin's spine, forced him toward the group who held Malmgren. He halted near Slattery, looking at the charred, still burning timbers. He brushed one hand across his forehead. 'All that money,' he said hopelessly. 'They had it planned so I'd suspect you, and I bit. Danged how I bit.'

Slattery walked toward the cabin. Shields handed over his prisoner and followed. He stared quizzically at Slattery, then let him in on some of the small talk he'd heard. 'Voss and Wells. Them too. They just dropped out in the dark. Dan'll put dodgers out on them.'

Slattery kept walking. The posse members who weren't holding prisoners had gathered at the fire, where they extended their hands to warm themselves. Some gave sidelong stares at Fenn's red shirt while they talked. Their guilt at allowing the shooting and treatment of the LeDucs had sunk in. No one made a joke or snide remark. A few had scattered, starting away for their horses as an excuse to get out of the group.

Shields said, 'I'll have a bank loan, Slattery. You need more cattle, I'll drive these into Montana for you.'

'I don't know, Mr Shields. My neighbors back home'll want the best price possible.'

'Sure, and I'll give it.' Shields watched him

carefully. 'Fourteen a head on the hoof.'

Slattery halted near the men who held Fenn and Trox. 'Put them on their horses,' he ordered. 'Tie them. I want to get back to the cave as soon as we can.' He pointed to the dead man. 'Take him along too.'

Charlie Shields rubbed his forehead. He kept his eyes on Slattery. 'What do you say? We've done business. I've set a price.'

'I figure Mr Crawford will set his price too, Mr Shields. I have to talk to him about this cabin. I'll let you know after.' Slattery left him and walked to where the posse was grouping the prisoners and horses.

CHAPTER SIXTEEN

Once the red arc of the sun topped the eastern peaks, the day grew terrifically hot. Before the posse had traveled a quarter-mile, the ever-present wind which blew down from the divide had cleared away all trace of smoke, leaving only a telltale odor to remind the men what they'd left behind. Mist steamed out of the tall grass, a thin, transparent whiteness that shifted and drifted in the slight breeze, hiding from view the red-winged blackbirds which bobbed and twanged among the reeds. Jays, scattered by the long line of horses and men, screeched in the brush and trees and flashed in steep swift dips through the yellow sunlight of the clearings.

Slattery halted the posse to breathe the horses at the first level stretch. Both men and animals were worn out from the sixteen hours of continuous moving. The men had said very little. Most of them kept to small groups of friends, and even there the talk had been sparse. Now, halfway up the rocky mountain trail, Tom Slattery glanced across his shoulder. The animals dragged along with a slow, choppy rhythm, one or two of the older and more tired clicking and stumbling under its riders' weight. The seven prisoners were in the middle. None had so much as made a try at escaping. They were as aware of the temper of the men as Slattery. The carbines and rifles had been returned to the boots. Reefers and stiff cowhide and bearskin coats had been taken off and draped and tied behind the saddles, yet the roughened faces, deep-lined, serious and thoughtful, were as watchful as ever. Their eyes narrowed, they kept their attention on the upper trail, their strong flesh tight to the cheeks and jawbones, the hands that fingered the reins close to the wooden stocks and coiled lariats hooked over the pommels.

Slattery had watched the trail above them just as much as the men he led. He couldn't see where the pass opened up toward the narrows and summit because of the overhang of the thick pine forest. He felt the immenseness of the mountains though, just as it had been felt during the night. Every so often he glimpsed through the branches the rearing uniform shadow of the peaks, the patches of snow glistening in the sunlight, standing out against the gray and black like huge pieces of torn white sheets. Slattery was staring up at the whiteness that covered one section of the rim when Augustin Vierra appeared in the trail ahead.

The heavy-set Mexican held a Winchester ready. He lifted one arm above his sombrero, lowered the weapon. Will and Bob Clark stepped from the timber fifty feet behind him. The three didn't smile while the posse approached. They simply stood without talk and waited.

Augustin said, 'We heard you. I was not sure it was the others coming back for the dead men.'

Slattery nodded to Augustin and the Clarks, who fell in alongside Charlie Shields and Wetterholm directly behind him. He could hear Shields begin to tell the father and son what had happened at the cabin. 'How is LeDuc?' he asked Augustin.

Vierra shook his head. 'Poor. Very poor. I do not know.'

'Marie?'

'If her father lives, it is because of her. She would not sleep, Tomas. She was beside him all the night. She is a fine woman, Tomas.'

159

The clearing that led to the cave opened ahead on the right. Marie LeDuc waited between the two middle boulders, watching. When she saw it was Slattery and the posse, she lowered the rifle she held and stepped back through the cave mouth. Augustin had heard the talk behind him. He said to Slattery, 'Malmgren, Rachins and Keelin? Quinn too?'

'Yes. And I wish there was a way to make them pay for Hager. How is he, Gus? He wasn't with Marie.'

'He just sits and says nothing. Except that he led the posse well.'

Slattery slowed King and drew up in the shade of the mountain. 'Give the horses a good rest,' he told Charlie Shields. 'Maybe Will and Bob'll give them a rub.'

'We'll rub them,' Bob Clark said. 'There's water higher up, Tom. We'll handle them.'

Slattery nodded. 'Thanks.' He stepped up the sandy, rocky incline past the boulders and through the high, wide opening.

It was cool, almost chill, inside the cave. LeDuc lay in the same position beside the small fire, the blankets covering him to his neck. His bearded face looked ashen, even in the semi-darkness. Alf Hager, in the rear of the large rock-walled room, didn't say a word. He stared blankly from Marie LeDuc to Slattery, then down at the cave floor.

Marie watched both Augustin and Slattery. She seemed very calm. She smiled from one

160

man to the other. 'I'm glad you're back,' she said quietly. 'You didn't lose anyone?'

'No. Has your father wakened?'

She nodded and wet her lips. Augustin had stepped to a large woodpile in the far corner. Marie watched his movements while he laid some sticks carefully on the low flames. 'He seems to breathe easier,' she said. 'I think he is stronger.'

Slattery saw now how tired she was, and that she was very pale. 'He'll have to be taken out in a wagon. I'll have one sent from Beaver Hole.'

'Not Beaver Hole,' she answered, frowning slightly. 'I don't want to go back there.'

'He needs attention, Marie.'

She bit her lips together and stared down at her father's slack, bloodless face. 'I can give attention here. Augustin has brought wood and water. And he will hunt for us.' Her face turned to the Mexican.

'I will stay, Tomas,' said Augustin. 'I will catch up with the cattle drive.'

The two of them, the Mexican and the woman, stood side by side, not touching one another, but somehow seeming as though they had been together for a long, long time.

'All right, Gus,' Slattery said. 'We'll be moving slow.' He stepped past them and walked to where Alf Hager sat. He hunkered down in front of the deputy.

'We'll be going back, Alf,' he said easily. 'You'll come with us.'

Hager's thin head nodded. 'I should be with you. I led the posse. I'll lead with you goin' back.'

'Alf, Charlie Shields will be in charge. I've got to ride to Crawford's ranch and talk to him.'

Nodding again, Hager grinned. The grin faded as soon as the smile wrinkles tightened his skin and hurt where he'd scraped his face. 'I'll lead, and Charlie'll go with me.'

Slattery rubbed one hand along the flooring, absently picking up a small pine twig. 'Charlie will lead, Alf.'

'No. No. I'll lead. Dan O'Hearn'll be watchin' for me. He expects me to bring them in. I'll lead.'

'Alf—' Slattery fingered the dried pine twig and exhaled with a quiet sigh. He realized he was pressing the point with absurd insistence. It would be rough enough on this little man once he reached home. He straightened, feeling the tired muscles of his back, shoulders and legs. 'You'll lead. I'll tell Charlie, Alf. I'll see you in Beaver Hole.'

He turned. Marie was bent over her father, smoothing out the makeshift pillow. Augustin was busy rearranging the woodpile that actually didn't need fixing. Slattery figured he'd wait until the posse and their mounts were rested, and then ride down to talk to Crawford. He'd been sent to buy cattle and get the best

162

price possible for the herd Lute Canby handled and any other steers which might be bought. He could do that and still catch up with Canby and the steers by tonight ... by tomorrow, because King needed the night's rest. He said to Augustin, 'I'll have Shields tell Lute, Gus. Take as long as you need.'

'I will, Tomas.'

Slattery moved toward Marie. She got to her feet before he reached her. She brushed her hair back from her small, serious face. 'I'll see Shields has more blankets and clothes sent up,' he told her. 'Gus will take good care of you. Both of you.'

'He will, I know. We'll be all right. My father will get better.'

Slattery nodded.

The cave was silent except for the sound of talk that came from outside.

Marie LeDuc looked at him gravely. She touched his hand. 'Thank you, Tom. We thank you.'

'I'll be back,' he said. She dropped the hand, and he smiled. 'I'll be looking for good news. I'll stop on my way back.'

Marie nodded. She moved toward Augustin. Slattery watched her say something to the Mexican. The two of them walked to where Alf Hager sat. When they spoke to the deputy and helped him stand, Slattery turned to go out of the cave ahead of them. He halted after a single step and dropped the pine twig into the fireplace. A few sparks flew up, and as he turned again to leave, a sputtering flame blotted out the spot where the twig had landed.

We hope you have enjoyed this Large Print book. Other Chivers Press or G.K. Hall Large Print books are available at your library or directly from the publishers. For more information about current and forthcoming titles, please call or write, without obligation, to:

Chivers Press Limited
Windsor Bridge Road
Bath BA2 3AX
England
Tel. (01225) 335336

OR

G.K. Hall
P.O. Box 159
Thorndike, Maine 04986
USA
Tel. (800) 223–2336

All our Large Print titles are designed for easy reading, and all our books are made to last.